BLOODLINE
Witch Cat Mystery: Book One

Tedeschi Publishing
294 S. Cedar Avenue
Wood Dale, Il 60191
Vickivass.com

Published in Print and Digital formats in the United States of America.

ISBN-13: 978-0692873311

Interior Format by The Killion Group, Inc.

Bloodline

Witch Cat Mystery: Book 1

VICKI VASS

To Terra and Pixel

Acknowledgments

Thanks to Karen Owen for the inspiration.

Thanks to Corinna Petry for her keen, journalistic eye.

And thanks to Michael Landon
for his beautiful cover illustration.

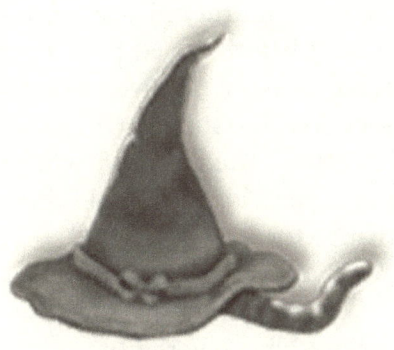

Salem, 1692

"RUN, TERRA." ELIZABETH'S SCREAMS REACHED me from within the barn. I could see the lanterns flickering like fireflies through the woods. "Run, run, Terra, now." Her frantic voice followed me as I darted through the thicket. Brambles cut through me, slashing at me as I pushed my way down the hill toward the stream. I could hear the hounds barking in the distance followed by the sounds of women screaming. The sweet goldenrod snapped beneath my feet, releasing the smell of licorice. Goldenrod, I thought, goldenrod ground with lavender brings on sleep. One of many concoctions Elizabeth had taught me. I hoped Elizabeth and the others had made it away.

My focus returned to my peril. I needed to keep moving. Holding up my skirt, I trampled through the tall grass and into the creek. The dogs wouldn't be able to track me through the water. Another trick Elizabeth had taught me. I pushed my way downstream past the hollow, avoiding the light coming from Master Johnson's farm. I followed the stream until I reached the sea, stumbling, falling onto the large rocks that jutted out like razors along the water's edge. The full moon gave me away, sparkling brightly onto the sea, lighting up the beach. I could hear them coming, the dogs barking, the loud, angry voices. I stumbled, panting. I was so weary. How long had I been running? It seemed like forever. I followed the shoreline until I reached a cove. My feet ached within my soaked boots, cut and bleeding from the rocks and thistles. I crept into a small cave and tucked deep into its corner. Covering my mouth with both hands, I tried to settle myself, but my heart pounded loudly. Surely it would give me away.

What had I done to cause such fury? I was only seventeen years old; some would say yet a child. A child, whose childhood was bled from her, taken by a thief. That thief told the secret. Life as I knew it would now change forever.

The Atlantic waters slashed clean and cool against the dark walls, the acrid smell of salt assaulting my nostrils. I stared out into the abyss. I could see nothing but the eternity that lay beyond the waters. What had they done with Elizabeth? Her screams continued to haunt me long after I could hear them. What would they do with me if I were found? I could hear voices in the distance, some real and some in my head. As of late, I had difficulty distinguishing betwixt the two.

I shivered from the cold. What of the others? What of Prudence, Sarah, Constance? Children of the coven, not much older than I. Had they been taken? Elizabeth would give her life to save ours. Was it their screams echoing in the distance? I had no means to save them. I reached into my pocket and clenched the small vial she had given me. A chance for a new life, a chance to save myself.

The voices grew nearer. I could hear their angry words; I could see the pitchforks through the flames, the bared teeth of the hounds. They were almost upon me. I drank the potion.

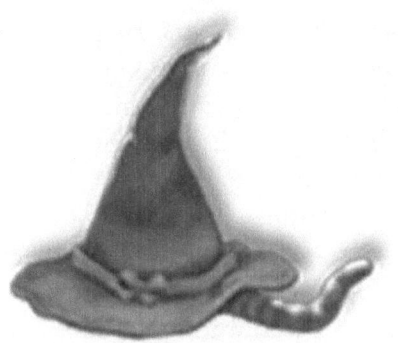

THE LEAF & PAGE

I STOOD ON THE STOOP OF the Leaf & Page, trying to ward off the early-morning chill. The crisp mountain air drifted down like a cloud over Asheville. Fall had rolled in seemingly overnight, bringing with it cool, damp mornings. I waited, shivering slightly.

"Come on in, dear." Mrs. Twiggs opened the back door to her tiny shop located in Biltmore Village, once home to the crafts-men and employees of the Biltmore Estate, the largest mansion in North America.

As she stepped over the threshold, the 125-year-old oak floors creaked under her plump feet. I followed her in through the kitchen and then into the store, winding my way along the display cases of crystals while she lit the incense burners scattered throughout the front room. Mrs. Twiggs was as dependable as a well-wound clock. She arrived precisely at five a.m. every morning to bake her scones and muffins before opening her shop of exotic teas and vintage books. She often said, "They're not going to bake themselves now, are they?" She always made enough to share with the others and myself. Myself always mindful to place first in line. "Oh, dear, you do look hungry. We'll fix that right away," she said, gazing at me, her hands on her wide hips.

"Thank you, Mrs. Twiggs," I said. She had told me to call her Beatrice, but it never felt right to me, not proper. Mrs. Twiggs, that's what I call her.

She scurried back into the small galley kitchen. I sat by the magnifying lamp that she used to examine her many crystals. Its warmth comforted me. From the kitchen I could smell bacon frying. "Almost ready, dear," Mrs. Twiggs called out to me. A few minutes later, she came out of the kitchen holding a Fiesta dinner plate bearing a slice of bacon and a blueberry scone. "Here you go, dear." She placed the plate in front of me. "Eat slowly. You don't want to upset your stomach."

Glancing up from the plate, I smiled and gave her a wink. I could hear the others shuffling in from the alleyway through the back door. Mrs. Twiggs greeted each one by name. I ate in silence, guarding my place carefully. As we ate, Mrs. Twiggs unpacked boxes of new arrivals, dusty books she had bought at an estate sale in Biltmore Forest, the small exclusive community that surrounded the Biltmore Estate. I accompanied her the day of the sale to make sure all the prices were fair. She has a kind heart, which some people use to their advantage. She held up each book like it was a revered first edition, carefully placing it in just the right spot on the sloping shelves. Like Mrs. Twiggs, the shop was in need of repair. Its floor slanted following the grade of the old cobblestone streets. The plaster walls peeled in parts, and the floor was scratched from years of wear.

After finishing my meal, I watched Mrs. Twiggs prepare the store for opening. She dusted the rows of wooden bookshelves located in the front room, the middle room was devoted to crystals and healing stones, and the back room held her selection of loose teas and herbal remedies. In the former dining room were several small café tables decorated with fresh-cut flowers from her garden. Upstairs, two tiny bedrooms, one filled with boxes, the other a double bed now serving as a single. A cozy cottage plucked from a Sir Arthur Conan Doyle novel, its keeper, just as quaint and proper. Mrs. Twiggs embodied all that is good about Asheville: kindness, sincerity, and grace. She turned the large kettle on to boil and began mixing her morning tea of the day. Each day featured a special brew, all secret recipes known only to her.

"Oh dear, look at the time," Mrs. Twiggs said, gazing at the antique cuckoo clock, which hung over the cash register next to the photograph of her late husband, Albert. She paused briefly, staring at Albert. "Good morning, dear," she said as though wait-

ing for him to respond. Albert Twiggs never answered her. In the
ten years that I had watched her morning ritual, he never uttered
a word, not that I expected a photograph to do so, but it would
have been nice to hear his voice. She waddled to the front door
and flipped over the open sign. All the others had left; it was up to
myself and Mrs. Twiggs to greet the first customers. She greeted
each with a hug and a smile. Mrs. Twiggs's warmth and generosity
endeared her to the community. The Asheville folk had accepted
her as their own, not their usual policy for anyone not born here.
Most Asheville-born families could recall several generations;
many as far back as pre-Revolution. Mrs. Twiggs doled out scones,
morning tea, and lively conversation about her favorite subject:
books. Before coming to Asheville, she had been a librarian at
the College of William & Mary, a place dear to my heart. I had
told Mrs. Twiggs my plans of attending W & M at one time, but
that time had passed. When her nose was not in a teacup, it was
in a book. She could speak on any subject, from ancient history
to Zen Buddhism. Of all the topics that interested her, Appalachian folklore was her favorite; that's what led her to the ladies
of the Biltmore Society and their monthly book club, which she
hosted at the Leaf & Page. The Biltmore Society was steeped in
tradition and secrecy. Its origins dated back to 1895 when the Biltmore Estate was completed. Mrs. Twiggs never mentioned what
occurred during the society's gatherings; I thought it rude to ask
since I am not a member, so I never did.

The silver bell over the transom tinkled, breaking my thoughts.
A woman I know as Mrs. Tangledwood came in, wielding her
crooked walking stick along the crooked floor. She was dressed in
a sensible coat, not indicative of a lady of her stature. She was wont
to save a penny where a penny could be saved. A longtime denizen
of Asheville society and the leader of the Biltmore Society Ladies,
Mrs. Tangledwood had been coming to the store as long as I have.

Mrs. Twiggs greeted her, easing her into the leather wing-back
chair nestled by the fireplace. "Emma, how are you feeling today,
dear?" Mrs. Twiggs spoke to the elderly woman with a concerned
air.

"Beatrice, my arthritis is acting up something fierce. I can feel
winter coming in my bones." She clenched her gnarled fingers as
she peeled off her quilted coat.

Mrs. Twiggs quickly gathered some kindling and started a fire, then said, "Let me get you a cup of tea." She bustled off and returned from the kitchen, carrying a tea service. She placed it on the small table. Placing several leaves in a strainer, she then poured boiling water over them, releasing an aroma I recognized.

"What is this, Beatrice?" Mrs. Tangledwood sniffed the tea.

"Emma, it's green tea with a bit of ginger, a touch of rosehips and willow bark. And something a little extra to take those aches and pains away, nettle leaves."

"What's nettle?"

I had used the plant myself for similar ailments. Mrs. Twiggs pulled up another chair and sat next to Mrs. Tangledwood. "It's a plant that has tiny stiff hairs that release stinging chemicals when touched; those chemicals numb aches and pains. The Appalachian mountain folk use it to reduce inflammation."

Mrs. Tangledwood stared at the concoction and then back up at Mrs. Twiggs.

"Oh, Emma, it's quite safe."

Mrs. Tangledwood sipped the tea. I could see her whole body ease, not from the tea but from the assurance in Mrs. Twiggs's voice. She had that effect on people. Her sparkling hazelnut eyes, her hair raven black without a trace of silver, and her tender smile. For a woman of almost eighty years on this planet, her skin was remarkably wrinkle-free and luminescent. She told me once that clean living and a purposeful life kept the gravedigger hungry. That must be true, for Mrs. Twiggs's purpose kept her young.

"One more thing, Emma." Mrs. Twiggs reached into her daisy-festooned apron pocket, retrieving a small crystal dangling from a piece of leather. "This is blue lace agate. It removes blocks from the nervous system and treats arthritic bones. I want you to wear it while you take a warm bath tonight for fifteen to twenty minutes." She placed the necklace gently over Mrs. Tangledwood's head.

Mrs. Tangledwood touched the stone and smiled. She opened her change purse, but Mrs. Twiggs waved her off.

"No, Emma, I want you to have this. You come back tomorrow and let me know how much better you feel."

"I appreciate it, Beatrice, you're quite kind, but I'm afraid that the report from my doctor's visit was not good. Even all your wonderful teas and stones can't cure what ails me. I'm afraid it's just a matter of time," Mrs. Tangledwood said, placing the teacup down.

Mrs. Twiggs's smile disappeared. She took Mrs. Tangledwood's hand in hers. "There's always hope, Emma. I will help you any way I can."

Mrs. Tangledwood smiled. "On to more cheerful business—the annual pumpkin festival at the Biltmore. I've spoken to several of the ladies, and we agree this year we should have a haunted hayride through the forest."

"Would you like me to speak with the curator at the Biltmore to arrange it?"

"That's not necessary," Mrs. Tangledwood said. "I've already spoken with her. They've agreed to allow us to use the woods for the event provided we donate the proceeds to their scholarship fund."

"Let me know if you need any help," Mrs. Twiggs said as Mrs. Tangledwood stood and buttoned her coat. "Emma—wait—it arrived. Let me get that book for you."

Mrs. Tangledwood sat back down in the chair with a groan. Mrs. Twiggs returned with a bundle and placed it on the table. "Emma, I'm afraid this one was very expensive. More than the others. It's quite old."

"Oh, Beatrice, how were you able to find it?"

"A colleague from the university back east."

"Thank you, Beatrice." Placing the bundle in her shopping bag, Mrs. Tangledwood stood again.

I watched Mrs. Tangledwood shuffle out the door with a newfound energy. Mrs. Twiggs closed the door gently behind her. Throughout the day, her patrons came and went, browsing through books, sifting through teas and sharing stories with Mrs. Twiggs. From my vantage point on the window seat, the afternoon sun filtered in through the beveled glass picture window, engulfing me in a prism of light. The sweet smell of afternoon raspberry zinger tea wafted in from the kitchen, filling the store with a sense of serenity. It would soon be overpowered by the scent of the expensive perfume worn by the ladies of the Biltmore Society as they pushed their way through the door. The shop would become a cacophony as the Asheville aristocracy pecked away the hours discussing matters of great importance. That would be my cue to part ways for the day for I am not privy to the hen party. The company

I keep is looked down upon by the ladies with turned-up noses, but not Mrs. Twiggs. She sees me for who I am and not what I appear to be.

I thanked Mrs. Twiggs and headed out the back door, making sure not to be seen. There was a chill in the air as dusk settled in. The days and my time grew shorter as winter approached. I needed to make arrangements for a warm bed for the night.

I made my way down Biltmore Avenue, heading uphill toward the downtown square. Outside the shops, the buskers played for the tourists. The locals sat at the outdoor taverns tied to their beloved dogs. Ashevillians love their dogs. I do not share their sentiment. They are dirty beasts with limited intelligence.

The Blue Ridge Mountains rose up in the distance surrounding the town, forming a fortress, silent, watching, waiting. I missed home, my real home, and a true New England winter. The Northeastern cold penetrates deep under your skin, nipping at all your senses. Large flakes of snow drift up to the window sash. Feather beds and warm fires call. Here snow is a fleeting promise, never staying more than a day and leaving no memory of its coming. I missed the taste of salt in the air and the sound of the Atlantic dancing with the moon tides. But of all things missed, I miss my family most.

I continued walking unnoticed through the crowds, listening to their chatter about their lives. Like many of my homeless kin, I am transparent, without substance. People see through me. Some turn their heads, not wanting to acknowledge I exist, others step out of my way. Yet there are those good-hearted folks like Mrs. Twiggs, more than not. Folks who offer tender mercies. They share their supper or a warm smile.

I arrived at my favorite haunt, the Fillmore Hotel, one of the last remnants of the Golden Age of Asheville located on the fringe of town. Scaffolds surrounded its exterior, masons working late into early evening. I love to watch the elegantly dressed people come and go. The women in their beautiful gowns, the men dressed in their finest suits, speaking of pleasantries and fine things. It had been longer than I remembered since I wore such fine clothing. The concierge, Wesley, greeted me. His slender frame adorned with navy-blue vestments, brass epaulets and buttons polished to perfection, his gray hair neatly cropped and brushed back with pomade. Unlike his gray hair, his pencil-thin moustache is kept black as night from the occasional dye, the only vanity he allows himself. He stands straight as a board as guests come and go. The sign of a proper concierge to be always ready, blending into the background never to be seen. With age comes tenure, allowing him certain privileges such as letting me in after hours to sit in the beautiful marble lobby to warm myself by the fire on cold nights. More of a reason to call Asheville home, people like Wesley who are always so kind and helpful. Even the well-heeled patrons of the hotel treat me kindly. Homeless? I'm not homeless. How can you be homeless when a town embraces you?

"There you are, miss," Wesley greeted me. "I was hoping you'd stop by tonight. I'll fetch you a bit of dinner."

"Thank you, Wesley, it is good to see you," I replied.

"You'll have to eat it around back. Too many guests, and they're already bothered by the construction. I hope you understand. I'll meet you in a few minutes," he said, nodding to a couple as they passed through the grand entrance.

It was nearly six p.m., and I had not eaten since this morning at Mrs. Twiggs. Sometimes I forget to eat. Other times a meal is hard to come by. I tapped on the servants' entrance. The solid wood door contrasted with its rough limestone exterior. The same masons who had transported the stones for the Biltmore Estate built this hotel. Wesley opened the door, holding an empty plate. "Miss, I regret I could not scrounge a single morsel for you." Wesley stared at the plate, bewildered and apologetic.

"Wesley, no bother. I could not eat a thing, stuffed I am. I dropped by on my way. It's just nice to see you." I glanced up to watch the sun setting over the distant mountains. I had to make it to the park before dark, otherwise he'd be gone and I'd have no place to sleep. I hugged Wesley and then turned out of the alleyway down the main street past the brewpubs coming to life and the strains of music spilling out onto the street. Small boutiques, artisan shops, and record stores flipped their signs to closed. Streetlights flickered on, giving a yellow glow to the darkening street. A line grew down the sidewalk for the Orange Peel as hipsters adorned with man buns and porkpie hats appeared like apparitions coming out of gangways and doorsteps. I hurried past them. Their conversations held little interest to me.

I hurried along the crooked streets into the Montford neighborhood. Of all the nooks and crannies of Asheville, this neighborhood was my favorite. The air was thick with the smell of moss and memories. A canopy of old-growth oaks wrapped their branches over the street. The houses teetered at the top of the hills, barely visible from the sidewalk hidden by lush green shrubs. Wraparound porches under high-pitched roofs and above heavy stone foundations held the weight of the hundred-year-old bungalows, Victorians, and Craftsmen homes. Like many of the older sections in Asheville, this neighborhood was the vision of the architect Richard Sharp Smith; the supervising architect of the Biltmore Estate. It's not possible to live in Asheville and not feel the presence of the Vanderbilts. I've heard all the stories, some true, some less than true.

Avoiding the man walking his pit bull, I entered the park. I meandered to where Lionel sat with his companions, playing chess. His grizzled white hair and beard lit up the dark skin of his face. He had told me how as a young man he walked for civil rights with the king. Now he walked with a cane. Old age hunts us all.

Lionel's companions were all about his age, seventy years young, he liked to say. They spent their days here challenging each other to chess and retelling stories of their youth. Each one topping the other. I listened until the sun was completely extinguished. Lionel pulled his torn and weathered overcoat close under his chin. "Okay, young miss, I think we better find a warm spot for the night. What do you think?"

"It's going to be a cold one, Lionel," I said with a little shiver.

I felt a kinship with Lionel. A kinship that living on the streets entitled me to. We walked past the boarded-up buildings, their broken windows stared like empty eye sockets. This part of town was not yet scheduled for gentrification. The bushes rustled with the night creatures scavenging for food. Lionel kept walking, seeming not to care; he knew these neighborhoods better than anyone. The streetlights and glowing neon from the bars lit our path. The sound of live bluegrass coming from one of the taverns followed us as we walked. I enjoyed country music, the twang of the fiddle, and the yodel in the voice. Lionel joked that the music in Asheville was not real country music. Real country music, according to him, came from the Deep South and wasn't called country. It was called blues, Delta blues.

Apart from chess, Lionel's other love was his guitar. Besides the coat on his back, his guitar was his only other possession. "I think this will be fine, first in line for Mrs. Twiggs," he said as he stopped in the alley behind the Leaf & Page. This side of the street was quiet, but I could still make out some chatter from the local wine bar across the street. I gave a shudder.

Lionel found us a warm spot between two dumpsters. Earlier in the day he had laid aside some comfortable cardboard and had rummaged for some blankets, well moving blankets actually. Probably left over from one of the out-of-towners moving to Asheville. They had been flocking to the mountains over the past several years, and an Asheville native was becoming an endangered species. I lay down against the wall, nestling through the blankets while Lionel pulled his guitar out of its gig bag. It was worn and weathered but came to life with the magic in Lionel's fingertips. "Young miss, this song is about a crossroads. Do you know what a crossroads is? That's a turning point in your life. Asheville is my crossroads, little miss." Lionel played his song for me, the same song I'd heard maybe a couple hundred times since the day I met Lionel. It always sounded slightly different depending on how he felt. Maybe it was the cold of the approaching winter, but tonight the song held a sadness to it that I had never heard before. An aching in Lionel's heart came through his fingers and out the guitar. I yawned. "I'm not keeping you up, am I, young miss?"

I shook my head no, too tired to answer, and then sleep found me.

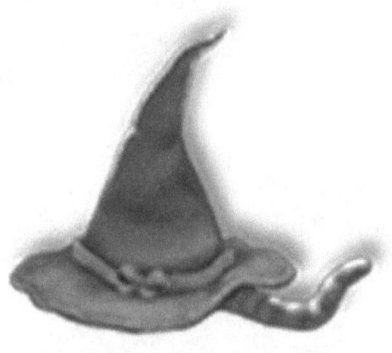

THE ALLEY

I WOKE UP AS THE SUN rose over the bluish smoke-filled mountains. I stretched and yawned. I glanced around for Lionel but didn't see him. Red and blue flashing police lights competed with the piercing sunlight for my attention. I went over to see what was going on. Two officers were questioning a young girl. I stayed in the shadows, eavesdropping. "I need to see your identification, your insurance," the older officer said to her.

"I don't have insurance," the girl said shifting from foot to foot. Her jeans were worn and full of holes, her T-shirt slouched over her shoulder, her long blond hair was tinged with pink. A tattoo covered her upper arm.

"What's your name?"

"Abigail."

"Abigail what?"

"Abigail Pierce." She opened the door of her rusty old car. The back seat appeared to be filled. I crept closer to get a better look and saw a sleeping bag, garbage bags filled with clothes and other belongings.

"You were sleeping in the vehicle last night?" the officer asked.

"Yes, sir. I just got into town and didn't have a place to stay."

The officer peeked inside the car and saw what I had seen. "You were here about three a.m.? In the alley?" he asked.

"I was out in front of the Wicked Weed performing until about two a.m.," she said. "That's when I noticed the guitar case on the passenger seat. And then I came to my car and fell asleep here."

"You didn't see or hear anything?"

"I was out. I drove ten hours straight to get here." She handed the officer her driver's license.

"You're from Chicago?" he asked, glancing at it.

"Yes, sir."

"You know you can't sleep in your car overnight. It's a violation of city ordinance."

"Yes, sir, I understand. I'll find a hotel today."

"We're going to need you to check in at the station when you find a place. We might have more questions," the officer said, handing her back her license.

"I told you I didn't see anything. Can I ask what this is about?"

The second officer spoke up, "A man was murdered in the alley last night."

"Lionel? Lionel?" I asked out loud. My heart skipped a beat. The officers turned to look at me. I ran down the alley and disappeared into the early-morning crowd.

I wandered the streets looking for Lionel until I found myself back at Mrs. Twiggs's shop. I didn't know where else to go. She knew Lionel. Maybe she knew where he was.

I knocked on the alley door. I knocked for a long while. Mrs. Twiggs opened the door, crying into her apron. She hugged me. "Lionel's dead. They killed him. Poor Lionel." I hugged her back.

"I am so sorry," I said, not having a comforting word to share.

Lionel had no enemies, just the opposite. Everyone who lived on the streets of Asheville loved Lionel. Listened to his stories, listened to his music. I looked over Mrs. Twiggs's shoulder and saw that girl the police had been talking to. She was sitting at the corner table, the one Mrs. Twiggs reserved for her favorite customers. Next to her were her guitar and her backpack, her most prized possessions I imagined. How was she involved with Lionel? What did she know? What did she see? Who was she? Something about her that bothered me, something more than the fact the police questioned her about Lionel. I kept my distance and listened carefully while Mrs. Twiggs brought over a cup of tea and sat across from her. "Thank you," the Abigail girl said.

"Everyone calls me Mrs. Twiggs."

"Mrs. Twiggs, I don't have any money to pay for this." The girl wrapped her hands around the warm teacup, cradling it.

"Don't worry about that." Mrs. Twiggs waved her off. "Do you have a place to stay? It's not safe to sleep on the street at night."

"I have my car. I'm saving enough money to rent a room. I've been playing to earn money," the girl said.

"You can play out in front of my store. I'd welcome that. Bring in more customers."

"You haven't heard me play yet."

Mrs. Twiggs smiled, glancing around the small shop. It was empty at this time of day. Only myself and one other customer browsing through the books. "Why don't we have a listen then?"

The Abigail girl pulled out her beat-up Gibson and played a song, the melody of which haunts me to this day. It was the same melody I heard as a young girl growing up in Salem. The words were different, but the music was eternal. I felt a dull ache in my head and what I imagined was vertigo. The room began to spin. There were voices all around me. It was dark; young girls squealed with joy.

"Constance, it's your turn," the giggling voice said.

"Sarah, help me."

"All join hands," Elizabeth said. We stood in a circle, clasping our hands together. Elizabeth stood in the center of the circle, her white flowing robe incandescent in the full moonlight, her pure white hair shone silver. Her green eyes cut through the darkness; her aura embraced us. I took a step back, releasing my hold on Sarah. "Terra, stop your silliness, join hands with the rest of us," Elizabeth ordered.

"Yes, Elizabeth," I replied, taking Sarah's hand again.

"Who will recite the seven incantations of the witch's oath? Constance," Elizabeth urged.

"I told you, Constance, it's your turn," Sarah said.

Constance closed her eyes, took a deep breath, and then recited from memory. "Only for good shall we use our powers, kept secret in shadows and midnight hours. Sisterhood joined never bond to break. Our bond is eternal, eternal our fate. We vow to hold sacred both nature and man and swear by the circle that we join with our hands. Protect all from evil for all earthly time. Stay true to our coven and preserve our bloodline."

"Very good, Constance," Elizabeth said. "Do you know what those words mean?" Elizabeth was our mentor. She was two years our elder, a young woman of nineteen, yet her powers were without equal. Her Oakhaven bloodline ran deep to the days of the Druids and beyond to the earth walkers before the humans appeared. "We have been gifted great powers. What we do with those powers decides who and what we are. There are some who would call what we practice the dark arts, but this is false. We are stewards of the humans, caretakers, who choose to do good with our abilities. As is true for all gifts of nature, those abilities come with a price. Each time you use your gift, a small part of you is drained. Spent is your vessel of white magic until you learn your true purpose. Until that purpose is known, you must spend your magic wisely." She paused. Her golden amulet flashed in the moonlight as she continued speaking. "There are many spells and incantations that I will teach you. I will show you the power of the herbs of the forest that will heal the mind and body." Elizabeth raised her arms as storm clouds rolled over the moon choking out its light. Lighting crashed across the sky, filling the air with the smell of sulfur. From a distance, her familiar howled. She levitated above us as time and our hearts stood still. And then she floated back to earth. "Tonight you must swear to me by this full moon that what you learn from this day forth you will use only for good." Elizabeth held up a simple silver chalice. "Constance, do you swear?"

"Yes, I do, Elizabeth." She took the chalice and sipped before handing it back to Elizabeth.

"Sarah?"

"I do, Elizabeth."

"Hester?"

"I swear with all my heart, Elizabeth."

"Prudence?"

"I swear, Elizabeth."

Each one responded in turn, following Constance's example. And then she turned to me. "And you, my brightest pupil, my dearest Terra?"

"Are you okay? You're shaking, what's wrong?" Mrs. Twiggs's voice brought me out of my trance. She was staring into my eyes. I couldn't speak. "What's wrong with you?" she asked.

I gazed up at her, brought back to reality. That Abigail girl was staring at me, not at me—through me. She had seen everything I had imagined in my head. She knew me.

She spoke. "What's wrong with that cat?"

"She has fits like that. I call them spells. They never last long; she will be fine," Mrs. Twiggs said.

"Is she your cat?"

"No, not really. She's been coming into the shop since I opened it. I fed her once, and now she keeps coming back." Mrs. Twiggs ran her hand along my soft fur. I arched my back, accepting her touch. Over the years, I've tried talking to Mrs. Twiggs. She's very intuitive in many ways. She can cast her own spells of sorts with her herbs and Appalachian remedies. But she never seems to understand me. This Abigail girl is a different creature. I think she can hear me.

Mrs. Twiggs and Abigail finished their tea. Abigail left, carrying her guitar. I meandered around Mrs. Twiggs's legs rubbing my fur against her to thank her for watching over me and caring for me. It was my only way to communicate to her how I felt about her friendship. By the smiles and the rubbing of my fur, I knew she understood and appreciated that friendship also. Now I had to go. I had to follow this Abigail girl to see who or what she was. I kept a safe pace behind her as she walked, her guitar case in hand, back to her car. She grabbed something from the glove compartment and then left. I hopped on the hood and peeked in the window, trying to get a better understanding of who she was. Like many of the street dwellers, both cats and people I've met in Asheville, she carried her home with her. I hopped to the back window and looked inside and only saw her clothes, some fast food wrappers. I followed the Abigail girl's scent down the sidewalks through the warehouse district, the seedier area of town, and saw her enter the pawnshop. As a customer opened the door, I snuck in to listen and see what she was doing.

"Excuse me, I have this watch I want to pawn," the Abigail girl said to the man behind the glass. She hesitated as she handed it to him. From what I could tell, it appeared to be an elaborately engraved silver pocket watch. It obviously held some meaning for her other than monetary.

Taking a loupe to his eye, the man gave it a quick once-over. "Fifty dollars," he said.

"It's worth much more than that. It's an antique," she argued, her face falling at the low amount.

"Just because it's old doesn't mean it's an antique," he said, trying to wind it. "It's broken. It doesn't even wind. Fifty dollars is a fair price, more than fair."

"I want to pawn it. I don't want you to sell it. I'll be back for it." The girl gave one last look at the watch as if reconsidering.

"If you're pawning it, I'll give you thirty dollars. You have ninety days to pick it up."

I tried to hold my concentration, but the gnawing sound from the corner kept pulling me away. I saw a fat field mouse that had found its way into the store. After centuries of being a cat, I had resolved myself to the fact that my meals would have to follow a cat's preferences. If you had told me the things I would find enjoyable as a cat when I was a girl, I would have said you were insane. But this mouse sounded and smelled delicious to me. This girl, this Abigail, would have to wait until I filled my belly. As I turned my attention to the mouse, I heard a voice say, "What are you doing here?"

When I turned, the Abigail girl was inches from my face, staring into my eyes. I said in my cat voice, "Who are you to ask me that?"

I shivered when she answered, "My name's Abigail."

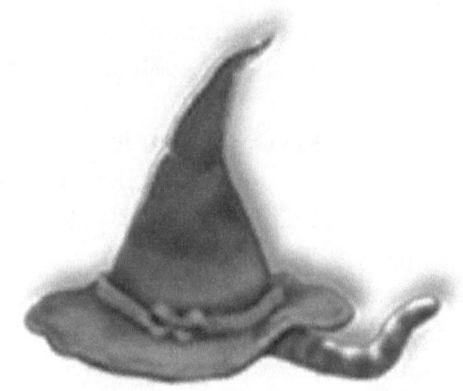

THE VOICES IN MY HEAD

THE ABIGAIL GIRL PICKED ME up by the scruff of the neck and pulled me out of the pawnshop. She carried me to a quiet corner of the adjacent parking lot. I dangled in front of her like a rag doll. If I had any of my old powers, I would have spent them on her in my fury. Instead I hissed and scratched her. "Calm yourself, cat. Why can I understand you? What are you?" she asked, shaking me.

"What am I? What are you? Why can you understand me?" I answered, continuing to struggle out of her grasp, clawing her arm with my sharpened claws. "For all these years, I've tried to speak with humans. But my speech has fallen on deaf ears."

She put me down. I surrendered to my cat instinct and started cleaning my fur, removing her scent. Then she spoke to herself out loud. "I'm having one of my episodes. I'm imagining this. I've been off my meds for too long." She counted the crumpled bills in her hand and walked across the street to the apothecary shop—that's not correct—in today's language it is called a drugstore.

I followed her. She went up and down the aisles, gazing at different bottles. I had learned to read in several languages and could understand the purpose of these potions. Most were derivatives of roots and herbs that I had gathered myself back in Salem. The Abigail girl picked up some cold medicine, antihistamines, and pain relievers. Then she walked down the naturopathic aisle and gathered Saint-John's-wort and Echinacea. The list went on. I watched carefully, realizing which potion she was creating. When I was an apprentice in Salem, I had watched Elizabeth give the humans who could not find sleep, potions with similar herbs, to calm the mind and take dreams away. The Abigail girl paid for her items and left never seeing me as I walked in the shadows. I had watched cats for hundreds of years walk like ghosts among the humans. They had many of the same characteristics as witches. I was too young at the time of my turning to have a familiar, but if I had, it certainly would have been a cat.

Elizabeth never finished my training. She also had not the time to teach me to turn myself back into a girl. On one hand, she saved my life, but on the other, she imprisoned me in this body. I had spent lifetimes searching for a way to return to my former self. The Abigail girl left the store and hid behind the dumpster in the alley. She crushed up the herbs and pills, spilling them into a water bottle she had bought. She shook the mixture and downed it in one gulp. She was trying to stop the voices in her head. That's when I said, "That's not going to work."

She jumped out of her skin, spilling much of the water bottle down her shirt. She turned to look at me. "You're not real. I'm not hearing you. The voices will stop in a while, and you will go back to being a cat."

"Abigail, I'm not a real cat."

Abigail poured the rest of her water over me. I hissed and ran off. I've learned to hate water. I shook my body, spraying the ground around me.

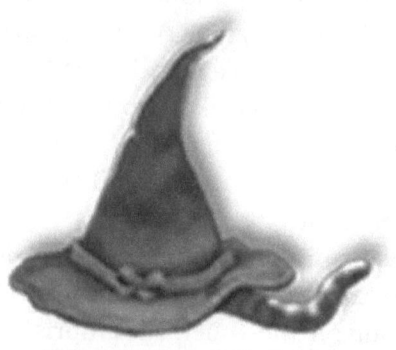

THE CABIN

AFTER DRYING MYSELF OFF IN the midafternoon sun, I took a quick catnap. I had forgotten all about the fat field mouse until I woke up and felt how hungry I was. I ran back to Mrs. Twiggs's tea shop, which overflowed with the lunchtime crowd. I wasn't allowed in when the humans were eating. I jumped up on the alley dumpster to peek in the kitchen window and scratched. Mrs. Twiggs looked up from where she was washing teacups in the kitchen sink. She opened the window. "Dear, what are you doing? You know it's not time for you yet."

I used my best pouting cat face. She reached up on her tiptoes and scratched behind my ears. I purred loudly and furiously, rubbing my head against her hand.

"Oh, okay, just this once." She grabbed me and pulled me in. "I've got some leftover tuna you can have." She fixed me a bowl, and I settled in. When I was done, I wrapped around her legs. As she turned to wash the lunchtime dishes, I jumped up on the table to study myself in a copper teakettle. I had been relatively attractive as a young witch. That feature I thought transferred to my cat body. My gray tiger-striped back and leopard-spot belly aren't so unusual for an alley tabby, but my eyes, green as emeralds, are clear and piercing. My facial features are soft and feminine. My whiskers dance when I purr and tumble. If I had to be a cat, this is the cat I wanted to be. Mrs. Twiggs caught me studying myself and chuckled. "You are such a little princess for a rough-and-tumble outdoor cat."

I looked up, blinking my eyes at her. She fixed herself a cup of tea and sat down. "You know, dear, I never gave you a name because I don't feel it is my place. A name is a very personal thing. I think a name says a lot about a person." She paused. "Or a cat." She sipped her tea. "You're always welcome here. In fact I wish you would stay with me all the time, but you don't seem that kind of cat. You're too smart for that nonsense. No, you are a free spirit."

I blinked at her again. Over the past ten years of our friendship, I tried to talk to her in blinks, hoping she would understand. I had spent hours learning Morse code from an old book I had found on her shelf. But poor Mrs. Twiggs didn't have the ability to understand me. She spoke to me out of loneliness, to hear her own voice, better than the silence of a dead husband. As much as people came and went in her life, the loss of her precious Albert could never be reconciled. I feel that heartache from Lionel's death. "Yes, dear, I miss Lionel too," she said. Maybe I was getting through to her. "Who would want to kill such a nice gentleman? A man who would never hurt a soul. A man who had nothing to give up except his life. I hope the police find who did this."

"If they don't, I will," I said.

Mrs. Twiggs merely smiled, not understanding my purrs and my noises. Or maybe she did? I gave her one last nuzzle and then headed back out into the streets.

I wandered through the crowds of tourists darting in and out of the stores. Sped by the local brewery where hipsters sat with their dogs on the patio. I heard a soft voice singing. It was Abigail. She stood outside the hundred-year-old general mercantile store, playing her guitar and singing. Her guitar case contained a few crumpled dollar bills in it. Even above the powering scent of perfumes and homebrew that poured onto the sidewalks, I could smell Abigail. I could smell her scent, but it was more than her scent. It was what Mrs. Twiggs called her aura, the colors that outlined Abigail. As a witch, I could see those colors around humans; as a cat, I could smell them. Her aura scent was different yet familiar. I had smelled it somewhere in my memory. The song she played that had put me in a trance was the melody my coven had sung the night before the witch hunters came for us. It was a very ancient melody dating back to what Elizabeth told us was the realm of the Druids. Many of the witches who came to America were from Scotland and Ireland. Their bloodlines dated back thousands of years to the spell casters who walked the earth from Samaria and the Nile back to the dawn of mankind and beyond. Our bloodline is ancient. Abigail's aura scent is ancient.

People walked past her, looking right through her like they do with me. Not acknowledging that she was a beating heart. In my three hundred years living as a cat, seeing people from this vantage point, I grew to appreciate and at the same time to be disappointed in humans. They could be both kind and cruel.

A drunk stumbled out of the bar, smashing into Abigail's shoulder. She righted herself, protecting her guitar. I listened in when he stopped to talk to the girl. "Hey, you're really good. What's your name? You're cute. How old are you?" He stood inches away from Abigail, shifting from foot to foot barely standing. His belly popping out from under his beer-soaked T-shirt. His greasy hair stuck against the sweat of his forehead.

Abigail politely said thank you and moved away. The drunken man moved with her. "No, I mean it. You're really cute." He reached for Abigail. She knocked his hand away. When she started to walk away, he grabbed her by the elbow and pulled her into the alleyway. I heard her yell. He pulled her into the dark. I ran after her, jumping on a fire escape as he put his hand over her mouth to stifle her screams. I leapt onto his back and clawed fiercely into the skin of his face. He screamed, "What's going on? What is that?" He fell to the ground in agonizing pain. His face contorted, changing shape, his eyes bulging and turning blood red. A voice not from this world came from his throat, "It comes."

Abigail picked me up, and we ran, grabbing her guitar on the way. When she finally stopped, breathless, we had reached the outskirts of Asheville by the Biltmore Estate. She fell to the ground sobbing. I pushed myself next to her, rubbing my scent over her. She ran her fingers along my soft fur. "What was that? Have I finally gone insane?" She stared into my eyes. "Was that real? Are you real?"

"Yes, Abigail, I'm real. Everything you've ever known or think you know is about to change. There are alternative worlds and creatures that walk between them. That creature in the alley was from the shadow world."

"What kind of creature are you?"

"My name is Terra Rowan. At one time I was much like you. Circumstance put me in this body, and powers I don't yet understand have bought us together."

"I'm too tired to understand this tonight. I have to find a place to stay." She rubbed her eyes, yawning and stretching.

I was exhausted as well; bringing her this far had taken much of my energy. "You can't stay on the streets. It's not safe anymore. I know a place. Follow me."

I led her into the densely forested woods between the oaks, ash, and thorn. These three trees are the magical trinity of the fairy folk. The mountain ash tree known as the rowan, my namesake, holds the power to ward off fairies and protect against black magic. As I've said, mine is an ancient bloodline. On my eighteenth birthday, I was to craft my wand from my ash spirit tree, the source of my power as a white witch. My wanding day never came.

Abigail tripped as the terrain became stubborn, not giving ground easily, I could tell she was exhausted. Asheville sits in a valley between the Blue Ridge, Appalachians, and Smoky Mountains. The mountain forests are thick with thorns and creatures that guard its entrance. Every step spends your strength and your will to continue; yet the Abigail girl did not rest. We headed toward the Black Mountain range so called because of the abundance of red spruce and fraser trees. At the summit lies a valley few have seen enchanted by the old ones. We followed the stream that runs from the French Broad River through the mountain. After some time walking in the dark, Abigail stopped. I had forgotten that humans don't have my night vision. She stood perfectly still. It wasn't the dark that stopped her, it was the feeling we were being watched. We hurried on at an urgent pace until we reached our destination. The Abigail girl stood looking over the old log cabin. "It's been empty for years since Agatha Hollows died. She took me in when I first came to Asheville," I said as she walked up the creaking steps. She peeked inside, holding her nose.

"It's not so bad. There's plenty to eat," I said as I heard a mouse scurry into a dark corner.

She looked at me. "How long has Agatha been gone?"

"She died shortly after the war."

She looked around. "What war?"

"The big war," I replied.

"Surely you can't mean World War II. You can't be that old."

"No, the war between the states. The Civil War," I said.

"The Civil War," she repeated. "How old are you?"

"I was seventeen in the year of our lord 1692." I thought for a moment. "So that would make me 325 years old."

"How is that possible?"

"I'm a witch. We age much differently than your folk. We have much of your same frailties; our bodies can't last forever, but we live much longer than humans. Until we reach our wanding age of eighteen, we age as you do. Once we wand, we stay young for hundreds of years," I explained. "That's why we live in secret, constantly moving from town to town. We must keep our secret."

"I'm too exhausted to understand this tonight. Please let's get some sleep." She found an old cot in the corner of the cabin by the fireplace. She was already sound asleep when I dropped the mouse by her feet. I made quick work of my dinner, and then I fell asleep next to her.

I woke up, leaving her still asleep. I owed it to Lionel to find out what happened to him. I headed back to town and to the alley to find the black-and-white stray I call Pippa. Giving names to animals reminds me that I am not one of them. Pippa frequents the alley where Lionel was killed. I found her sitting by the alley's entrance, begging from passersby. She was a tuft of a mutt no more than ten or eleven pounds with curly, matted fur. Her eyes are kind, her disposition sweet. She is a tolerable dog by my belief. "Pippa, did you see what happened to Lionel?"

"I wasn't there." She wagged her tail.

"Have you heard anything at all?"

"The fat orange cat." I knew which fat orange cat she was talking about. I'd seen him scrounging for food, constantly on the move. Throughout my centuries as a cat, I learned to communicate to animals telepathically through images. Cats were the most tele-pathic of all; they usually understood quickly. Dogs are arrogant. They dislike cats and struggle with the concept that I can com-municate with them. Another reason I began naming the animals that lived on the street. It helped them accept me as a friend. I had never spoken to the orange cat, but I knew he'd be where food would be found. The large tomcat was outside the Dunkin Donuts, rummaging through a garbage can. All I could see was his fluffy hind side sticking out of the trash bin as his long tail wagged ferociously. He popped his head out of the garbage with a half a donut on his head and hissed at me. "Hush up," I said.

He didn't understand. "Do you hear me talking to you?" He turned his head sideways, looking very confused and stupid.

That's when I realized he wasn't the brightest cat in the alley. I began to talk slower. "Do you understand what I'm saying?"

"Me," he replied.

"Okay, what does that mean?"

He shook the donut off his head. "Me," he said again, nibbling at it.

I looked into his thoughts. In them he was lying on his back, eating a piece of pizza surrounded by discarded hotdog buns. "You're hungry?"

He shook his head and said, "Me hungry."

"Okay, we have that settled. I can catch you a delicious mouse," I said, showing him an image of a mouse.

Mouse he understood and jumped out of the garbage dumpster to rub against me and bite my neck. "Me hungry, me hungry, me hungry, me hungry."

"What should I call you? We need to establish names first. My name is Terra. Can you say Terra?"

"Me hungry Terra."

"Okay, very good. Now what do you look like? What is your name? Your name is very important. It says a lot about who and what you are. It gives you a presence, a place. It leaves behind who you were. We must choose a name that is appropriate."

I looked around, but he was gone. "Orange cat, where did you go?" I walked down the alley, searching for him.

I could see his silhouette through a cracked stained glass window lying in a pile of furniture. He looked fuzzy, pixilated. He smiled his pixilated grin at me. "Pixel, that's your name."

He popped his head out from around the window. "Me Pixel, Pixel," he repeated.

"You are Pixel, we established that. Were you in this alley the other night?"

"Me Pixel."

I sighed. "We're going to have to work on this." Using my telepathy, I showed him an image of Lionel. He understood.

"Did you see what happened to Lionel?"

Pixel didn't understand.

"Did you see bad things?"

There was something blocking his thoughts. I couldn't see them. I thought at first it was his inability to summon up images, even basic ones like the other cats. It was more than that. He was hiding something. "Pixel, let's get you something to eat."

"Pixel hungry," were his final words as he followed me.

Pixel and I headed back to the cabin. The Abigail girl was waking up. She hadn't eaten any of the mice I had left her. So I ran to the stream and caught several fish. I threw one to Pixel who made short work of his. I carried the other triumphantly to the Abigail girl. She found flint strike and started a fire. She gathered up some twigs. She cleaned the fish. Pixel waited for his share patiently by the fire. "Who is this?" she asked.

"This is Pixel," I told her.

"Me Pixel," Pixel said, pleased with himself, puffing up his white chest.

She appeared surprised. "I can understand him too."

"You're hearing him through me."

"Oh, of course, I forgot. You're a witch," she said.

"Witch?" Pixel asked.

"Don't worry about it, Pixel," I said before turning to the Abigail girl. "I think Pixel knows what happened to Lionel, but he's not telling."

She gave Pixel a stern look. Pixel cleaned his paws and then his belly, rolling over on his back, rocking back and forth in his ignorant bliss.

"Don't mind Pixel, he's not very bright."

"What did Pixel see?"

"It's not what he saw, it's what he heard. He keeps humming a song that Lionel played, a Delta blues song."

"Lionel was a musician?"

"Yes, a very talented guitar player, singer, songwriter much like yourself."

She smiled. "Thank you, I appreciate that. Not too many people have said that to me."

"Lionel played a song for me the night he was murdered."

"Sing me the melody. What are the lyrics?" she asked.

"The world is turning while the angels keep watch. It's the last line I heard before I fell asleep. That's what has been bothering me. I don't know how I could sleep through…" I hesitated feeling a sudden guilt. I could have saved him. I could have fought off whoever did that to him. Something or someone kept me asleep.

She repeated, "Angels keep watch. It does sound like a Delta blues lyric."

"Lionel loved the blues. He said he had swamp water running through his veins."

"I think I would have liked Lionel," Abigail said.

I nodded. "Lionel was very humble. Even though he was a man of means at one time, he chose to live on the streets."

"Why would he do that?" she asked.

"Lionel watched over people."

"What do you mean watched over people?"

"All beings have a purpose. Some are given that purpose, others find it. Lionel found his, he took care of people. The people who need the most care are the street folk. He made sure we had a place to sleep, food to eat. He kept us safe. He was able to do that because people trusted him. I don't think he would have earned that trust if he hadn't lived amongst us."

"I don't understand."

"To understand Lionel you have to understand where he came from," I said. "He was a preacher from a small parish in Louisiana, a leader in the community. It could have been any small town in America where hardworking folks attend church on Sunday. A family of sorts and Lionel their father." I paused, remembering Lionel sharing his stories. "But under that idyllic parish lay a darkness, a curse. There are places in this world that keep a dark silence, a knowing you might say. Lionel's parish was such a place. Members of his congregation started disappearing. At first they thought it bad luck. The swamp is a dangerous place in itself, but the bayou folk know differently. They understand black magic. They have a name for when evil takes good folk. They call it the reckoning. But life continued as it must. On Sunday he preached God's mercy to a dwindling congregation. He kept the faith for the faithful and gave his parish hope. Whatever magic was in Lionel saved his parish. A few years later, he fell in love and married. When he learned she was with child, he nearly burst with joy so he said. His joy was short-lived because his young bride died giving birth to his child. And his first born, a boy child, was stillborn. The reckoning came for Lionel, and then the rains came; it took his parish, it took his aunt and uncle. It took everyone Lionel knew. The levee broke and took them all. The reckoning took them all, leaving only Lionel behind."

She sat down in the rocking chair beside the fire. I jumped up on her lap and began to purr, an emotion I couldn't control. "I can't accept what you're telling me," she said.

"I told you your reality is never going to be the same. There's a lot of magic out in the world. Not all of it is good. You can choose to accept it or pretend it doesn't exist. That doesn't change the fact that it's there. The reckoning followed Lionel. It took his life."

"Me tired." Pixel interrupted. He lay down next to the fire, rolling back and forth on his back, wagging his tail. Bright orange and blue aura colors radiated from the fat orange cat, the essence of peace and kindness. He was a kind cat. Whatever he knew about Lionel's murder, he would tell us in time.

The Abigail girl gazed around the cabin, seeing its dusty floors, dirty windows, and the cobwebs hanging from the ceiling. "This could be a nice place." She walked around, the floorboards creaking. I followed. Stepping outside, she went to the small outbuilding where Agatha Hollows kept her herbs and medicinals. The small vials were dusty, drenched in the same cobwebs as the cabin. "What is all this?"

"Agatha Hollows was a healer. The mountain people came to her for all their ills. This is where she kept her medicine."

Abigail picked up a jar of sage, opened it, and took a whiff.

"She taught me how to use the local herbs to make potions. I know which ones can help with your headaches," I said.

"Can you stop the voices?"

"The voices are real, Abigail. You can only stop them by listening to them."

She ignored me. It took me many years to accept the voices I heard. Abigail sat down on a small stool by a rack that held jars of dried herbs. She opened one and pulled out the herbs. They were brittle from drying too long. She took them in her hands and breathed them in.

"That's digitalis. The kind woman used it for patients who had heart problems."

I watched her, trying to determine who she was. As of yet, I had not teetered to one side or the other.

We spent the day tidying up our new home. Brought together by circumstance and need, we were becoming a family. I studied the Abigail girl as she cleaned. She hummed softly to herself while Pixel danced around her. She was no stranger to hard work. Pixel was a little more reluctant. He was perfectly happy, tumbling about, looking for mischief and food. I sent him into the woods to hunt for our supper. I watched him scamper off, belly wobbling, scraping the floor. He made a fine dust broom. His orange-striped tail disappeared into the blackberry bushes.

By twilight Pixel returned with a rabbit, which he dropped at Abigail's feet. He sat and watched her clean and cook it, never taking his eyes off his kill. "Me hungry," he moaned. By darkness air turned cold, and then we heard the howling.

Pixel flew to the windowsill. His tail bashing back and forth frantically, making little growling noises, answering whatever it was that hunted us. Whatever it was, it kept sure to stay in the shadows.

"Is it a wolf?" Abigail asked.

I shook my head no. I could smell its aura. It was very old and very evil. It was not of this world. Before I could warn Pixel, he slipped out the front door and headed into the darkness. Abigail yelled, "Pixel, no." I threw myself at her feet, tripping her before she could reach the door. And then I ran out to help him.

I splashed over the stream, darted through the overgrown blackberry bushes, which snagged at my fur, following the scent of the creature. I could hear Pixel screaming farther up the mountain. "Pixel, save, Pixel, save," his words came out as quick gasps. I ran as fast as my four legs could take me until I reached a clearing where I found Pixel lying on his side, bleeding. I covered his body with mine, swiveling my head back and forth, searching for the unknown creature who had done this to my friend. "I save Terra," Pixel whispered.

"Yes, you did, Pixel." I picked him up by the scruff and carried him back to the cabin, stopping in the stream to wash his wounds.

That's when I saw a pair of red eyes glowing from the woods. I backed up slowly, pulling Pixel onto the bank of the stream. Elizabeth had told me that dark creatures couldn't cross over moving water. That's why the good are baptized in water to defend against evil. And that's why Agatha Hollows built her cabin by the stream.

Abigail ran out of the cabin, lifting us both off the ground, pulling us in and locking the door behind her. "What was that?" she said, looking over Pixel's wounds. She tore a piece of her T-shirt and stanched the blood from the worst of them. She began to boil water in the hearth.

"Pixel, fine. Me okay," he said with a brave heart.

Exhausted by the battle, Pixel flipped over near the fire and fell asleep. Abigail glanced at me as she finished cleaning Pixel. "What was that, Terra?"

I had no answer. I simply said, "You sleep now. I'll keep watch." I climbed up to the windowsill, staring out into the darkness.

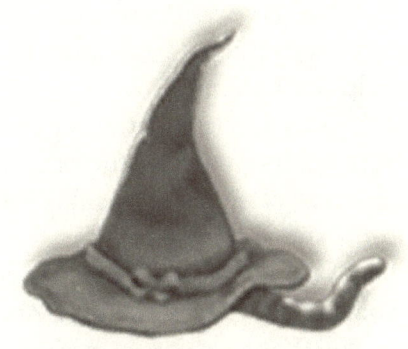

MORNING BREAKS

I KEPT A STEADY WATCH THROUGH the night. With the sunlight came safety. Dark creatures prefer the cover of darkness. I could hear Pixel talking in his sleep behind me. "Me hungry," he said repeatedly. Apparently, even in his dreams food is foremost on his mind.

Abigail stoked the fire and pulled the chair up to the window next to me. "Terra, what happened last night?"

"Whatever creature it was, it was malevolent. Its smell was muddy and putrid."

"What are you talking about?"

"Abigail, whatever it was is gone. Today we will make preparations to ensure it never returns."

"I need some caffeine like really bad. Let's head into town," Abigail said, standing up.

I nudged Pixel to wake him up. He stood, stretched, and emitted his Pixel noise, a combination of happy growls and hunger cries. "I know, Pixel."

"Pixel hungry."

"We have to hurry to make it to Mrs. Twiggs before her store opens. She'll have plenty for you to eat."

We made our way back down the mountain. Out of the corner of my eye, I saw something tracking us. Every so often a flash of red and white would break through the green of the trees. It was not the creature from the night before, but I could not be sure of its intention. I urged my companions to hurry. Pixel heard it also above the rumbling of his tummy. I was amazed how fearless this fat orange alley cat was. He was determined to make Mrs. Twiggs before her store opened, and no bear, boar, or dragon could stop him. I couldn't help but to smile.

As we entered the city limits, our tracker disappeared back into the forest. We reached Mrs. Twiggs as the others were already lined up by the garbage cans, cats and dogs alike. She tried not to play favorites, but I knew she was a cat person.

Mrs. Twiggs peeked out the kitchen window into the alley. When she saw Abigail, she opened the back door. "Dear, I've been so worried about you. Your car's been parked out front all night. Where have you been?"

"Mrs. Twiggs, it's a long story but one that would tell better over a cup of tea. If you don't mind?"

"Certainly, dear, come in, sit by the fire." Mrs. Twiggs led Abigail into the front room and sat her in the chair where Mrs. Tangledwood had rested the day before. Pixel and I snuck in, sticking close on Abigail's heels.

Mrs. Twiggs brought out plates of crumbled raspberry scones, bacon, and whatever lunch was left from the day before to the back alley. I heard the others meowing and barking happily as she fed them. When she came back inside, Pixel meowed and circled around Mrs. Twiggs's feet. "Abigail how did these two get in?"

"They're with me," Abigail said.

"I don't recognize this orange tomcat."

"They stayed with me last night in a cabin up on Black Mountain."

"Oh, Abigail, I better fix myself a cup of tea first. This sounds like quite a tale." As Mrs. Twiggs served tea and breakfast, Abigail began reliving our previous night. Mrs. Twiggs quietly listened, absorbing each word, nodding politely, adding extra sugar cubes to her Earl Grey. As Abigail continued, so did Mrs. Twiggs's addition of the sugar cubes. I counted ten in all. When Abigail had finished, Mrs. Twiggs finished her tea and slowly returned it to its saucer. She sat quietly for a moment, pondering, and then spoke. "Abigail, dear, that's quite a story." I could tell by her inflection that she did not believe a word Abigail said. "Dear, if you need help, there's a free clinic downtown that helps people in these situations."

"What kind of situations?" Abigail sat up.

"You're obviously overtired, distraught. The mind can play tricks on a person," Mrs. Twiggs said.

"Mrs. Twiggs, I'm not crazy."

"No, dear, I never said you were crazy. I don't think that at all."

"Well, that's what you implied."

"Dear, don't be upset." Mrs. Twiggs reached out her hand and patted Abigail's arm.

Abigail stood up. "Thanks for breakfast." Then she walked out the door, Pixel and I following behind.

"Abigail, Mrs. Twiggs is a good woman. She's only trying to help," I said.

"She thinks I'm crazy. Why shouldn't she? I think I'm crazy. I'm talking to a cat."

Pixel stared up at Abigail with his big orange saucer eyes and meowed. "No offense, Pixel," Abigail said.

"We're going to need some supplies. How much money do you have left?" I asked.

Abigail checked her pockets. She pulled out two one-dollar bills. Then she reached in her other pocket and pulled out the keys to her car. "I don't have money for gas. I can't pay the parking tickets, and I can't sleep in it overnight."

We left the used car lot with $150. "We need some food for you. Pixel and I can catch what we need. There are some herbs and spices we'll have to purchase," I said.

Abigail looked down the street toward the Leaf & Page. "We best go somewhere else." Pixel and I waited outside the Ingles supermarket. I recited to Abigail a list of herbs that we needed. After she picked everything up, we returned to the cabin. She placed the bags on the small wooden table by the potbelly stove. "Okay, Terra, you want to explain what all this is?"

I leapt up on the table and nuzzled the small box of cloves. "The clove is a very powerful protective against evil spirits." Then I nuzzled the cumin. "The cumin we mix with the salt."

Pixel tried to leap on the table, failed, and sat on the floor watching, licking his wounds.

"Abigail, I'll walk you through it. Equal parts salt and cumin sprinkled on the windowsills and doorway stops evil from entering. Also place the dill above the front and back door." I stared out the window intensely. Every once in a while I saw the same flash of red and white through the blackberries. It was a blur.

After she had followed my instructions, Abigail picked up garlic cloves and gave me a sarcastic look. "Tell me this isn't for vampires, Terra."

"No, don't be silly. There's no such thing as vampires, but it does work against shape shifters, raccoons, and black magic."

"Raccoons?"

"From that sentence, you took away raccoons?"

Abigail laughed.

"Raccoons are mortal enemies of cats. I'd prefer the shape shifter and black magic over a raccoon."

"Pixel too."

"Is this really going to keep away whatever was out there last night?"

"We need to gather some more herbs, twigs and berries from the forest, to make a wreath of blackberry and rowan."

"Your namesake, right?" asked Abigail.

"Yes, the mountain ash tree. There are several around the cabin. Agatha Hollows planted these trees to make protective wreaths for the mountain folk. Because the ash tree is my spirit tree, it makes the talisman even more powerful."

We spent the day outside gathering what we needed and fashioning our talismans. As I picked the blackberry and its leaves, I was careful not to give notice to our tracker that I had seen him. As of yet, I did not know his intentions but thought that if they were bad, he would have made them known by now. Instead he just watched. Pixel came up behind me, growling. "I know it smells like a dog, Pixel, but I can't be sure," I told him.

"We go now," Pixel said.

We returned to the cabin. Abigail had laid out cans of tuna. She was scratching her hands.

"What's wrong?" I asked.

"I must have touched something that irritated my skin. Maybe it was poison oak or sumac."

I saw the nettle leaves in her basket by the dandelions. "Why did you pick those?"

"I don't know. I felt like we should have them."

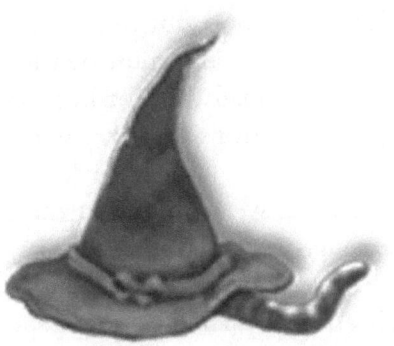

NETTLE LEAVES

NETTLE LEAVES. MRS. TWIGGS USES them for aching bones. Elizabeth also used them to capture curses and send them back to the caster. There's more to this Abigail girl than I first thought.

After eating her supper, Abigail pulled out her guitar and strummed it softly. Pixel wrapped his way around her feet, then finally settled on his back in front of the fireplace. I felt we were safe and yet occasionally turned a watchful eye to the window. I allowed myself to relax, finally drifting off while Abigail's melody played in my head until I wasn't sure if it was Abigail playing or not. The music grew louder. The choir finished its hymn; I sat on the hard wood pew, struggling to keep my eyes open as Reverend Samuel Parris stepped up to the pulpit.

"The lord watches over us in these troubled days. He tests us with temptations of the flesh as we see in Salem town. With prosperity comes pride, one of the seven deadly sins. I look around me. I see hardworking farmers, good Christians who believe that hard work and sacrifice is the way to heaven. Make no mistake, the devil walks amongst us. Thou must shun the ways of pride."

Prudence whispered in my ear, "He's jealous because the townspeople have bigger houses, finer clothes, and more prospects than us poor villagers."

"Shh." I quieted Prudence before the tithing man could tickle us with his wand of foxtails. To talk in church meant punishment by his hand. I glanced around at the congregation dressed in their plain wear and white bonnets. I adjusted mine. Elizabeth, even in the simplest of clothes, stood out from the other young women. Her beauty was undeniable and must be the reason the reverend's apprentice Jonathan Goodall vied for her attention. Elizabeth had told me once of his intentions to marry her, but that meant giving up all who she was.

When service ended, we gathered in the courtyard filled with spring lilacs releasing sweet perfume.

"What of tomorrow?" Prudence asked.

"Prudence, Elizabeth's warned us not to speak of that day," I said, giving a furtive glance around to ensure that no one was listening.

"I don't understand why all the secrecy."

"You know that the elders have forbidden the May Day celebration," I whispered.

Finishing her conversation with the young Goodall, Elizabeth came over to us, a small smile gathering on her face. "Terra, Prudence, you were causing quite the commotion in service. Prudence, I've spoken to you about such behavior. We should not be drawing unseemly attention to ourselves. With last year's poor crops, rumor has spread of witches amongst us."

"Everything bad is blamed on us. If someone stubs his or her toe, it's a witch. If a child has a bad dream, it's a witch. When will these mortals take responsibility for themselves?" Prudence said.

Elizabeth grabbed Prudence by the arm firmly, pulling her behind the lilacs. I followed. In a hushed voice, Elizabeth commanded, "Do not speak of these things. Do not act out. You're endangering all of us."

"Yes, Elizabeth, of course." Prudence stared down at the ground at her black shoes adorned with inappropriately oversized silver buckles. Her skirt had covered her indiscretion.

Elizabeth noticed them too. "Prudence, I told you never to wear those."

"No one can see. They make me feel good. Why shouldn't I have nice things like the townsfolk?" Prudence asked.

Elizabeth's smile disappeared.

I felt something brush against my face, followed by a scratch like sandpaper on my ear. I could feel my arms and legs turning into paws, my skin to fur. I was no longer a young girl. I woke to find Pixel curled up on me, cleaning my ear.

I could smell bacon frying in the old cast-iron pan. "I made breakfast and some tea. Do cats drink tea?" Abigail asked.

Pixel jumped up, not understanding but smelling the food in the air. "Me hungry. Me hungry." He circled around the cabin, his tail wagging ferociously.

I jumped to the table and sniffed the tea. It had a distinct musky minty smell. "Abigail, is this nettle tea?"

"Yes, I added some nettle leaves to the green tea."

"Why would you do that?"

Abigail stopped and thought for a moment. "I don't know."

"Abigail, what are you doing in Asheville? Why did you come here?"

She took the bacon out of the pan, plated it, and sat across from me. Pixel reached up her leg, trying to get to the bacon. She lifted him up to the table. While he devoured his meal, Abigail said, "I told my parents I was hearing voices in my head. At first they thought it was a young girl's nonsense, but as I grew older, the voices became stronger. They shuffled me between doctors. Finally they took me for an MRI. I overheard them telling the doctor that they didn't know my family history because I was adopted. When I confronted them about the adoption, they didn't want to talk about it. They handed me the pocket watch and said it belonged to my real parents. I was so angry I left, and I haven't spoken to them since." She paused. "I think the voices are my real parents, but I can't remember their faces."

"What do the voices say?"

"They told me to come to Asheville to get down to the cross-roads."

Crossroads, I thought. Lionel believed Asheville was his cross-road. I curled up on the chair, pondering that word and what it meant for him, for her, for them.

Abigail stood and walked to the sink to clean the dishes. Pixel dropped a mouse at Abigail's feet. She bent down and scratched his back. "Thank you, but I'm full from breakfast."

Pixel grinned up at her as the mouse scampered to safety. As Pixel helped Abigail clean the dishes, I rummaged through her garbage bag suitcases, going through her clothes, looking for clues of who she was, why she was here and how she was connected to Lionel. I usually have great intuition when it comes to these matters, but the trust I had placed in Abigail was dwindling. She was parked near the alley where Lionel was murdered. She knew more about potions than she let on to me. For good or bad, something drew her to Lionel, and perhaps because of it, Lionel was dead.

I stepped outside onto the wooden porch, overlooking Black Mountain. Morning dew stained the wood floorboards. There were massive paw prints leading to the front door and then a dry spot where something had settled for the night. I could smell our tracker. Pixel was right; he smelled like a dog. "Me, right," Pixel exclaimed from behind me.

"How did you sneak up on me like that? I didn't hear you."

"Me quiet," Pixel whispered, biting my ear.

We followed the paw prints that circled the cabin. Pixel dug into the fresh dirt around back. He proudly presented me with some sticks, which I recognized as ash, thorn, and oak. Pixel scurried to another freshly filled hole and retrieved the same. This continued around the entire perimeter of the cabin. Pixel sat with a twig in his mouth and a confused look. "This combination of sticks is good magic, Pixel. White magic. It protects anyone within the cabin," I told him. No dog would know to do this.

"Pixel, Abigail," he said.

"No, not now, Pixel, let's keep this to ourselves until we find out who this tracker is." I stared off into the distance but didn't see any sign of our tracker. Pixel flopped over onto the grass and rolled around in mad circles. I am constantly amazed at his joy in simple pleasures.

Abigail stepped onto the porch, holding her arm up to shield her eyes from the midmorning sun. I saw her. Until now she had been the Abigail girl, the human who was to lead me to answers I was seeking, but now I really saw her. She is an incredibly beautiful girl. Her platinum hair turning almost absolute white in the bright sun, giving her an ethereal quality. She is tall, much taller than the young girls of my time. Her slender features and pale skin would make a Tolkien elf envious. There is something very elfin about her, the way she carries herself, the way she walks through the forest as though she had walked here hundreds of years ago. A nimbleness to her step. She sat on the edge of the stairs, staring off at the same distance I had myself several minutes ago. She was searching for something.

I sat down next to her. That's when I got a closer glimpse at the scar that ran down the back of her arm, which was covered by a tattoo of Tinker Bell.

She caught me noticing it and covered it with her other arm. "Cat, what are you looking at?"

"Nothing," I said, turning my back to her. Pixel scampered up the steps, jumping into her lap with his guttural happy noises. "Today is Lionel's funeral. Myself and the others will be watching from the edge of the cemetery. We're not allowed in when the humans are about. You're welcome to come."

Abigail nodded her agreement. As Pixel and Abigail started down the path to town, I ran into the cabin and retrieved the remaining bacon Abigail had made. I placed it outside the front door for the tracker. By nightfall, we should know his intentions. Either way, I prepared myself.

A short while later, we entered the large iron gates of Riverside Cemetery, located deep within the Montford neighborhood. Lionel had talked about the cemetery in his last days as if he knew he would soon be a resident. He told me, "Bury me in the rolling hills overlooking the French Broad River. My people helped build this town, this cemetery; some of them are buried here. I want to be near family."

Walking among the headstones, we passed Thomas Wolfe and O. Henry, famous literary figures who had called Asheville home. I realized I didn't know Lionel's last name. To everyone on the streets, he was just Lionel. Abigail stepped quietly through the headstones, not noticing names. Pixel ran off chasing a squirrel. A crowd gathered by a freshly dug grave along the water. I wonder if Lionel knew that dark creatures couldn't cross over moving water. Was that why he wanted his grave by the river? He had told me that the French Broad River was a powerful force. It is the second oldest river in the world, only the Nile is older. It had a good mojo, Lionel said. It defies nature because like the Amazon and Nile, it flows in a northerly direction. Lionel said it starts deep within the eastern continental divide where the world split apart, good on one shore, evil on the other. Maybe he did know. Maybe he did know that evil can't cross moving water.

Abigail walked up to the back of the crowd, blending her way into the dark clothed mourners. I hid behind a headstone and listened to the preacher start his eulogy. He spoke with the same cadence as Lionel, a mixture of Cajun and Southern drawl with a smearing of French. "I knew Lionel. He was a good man. Many days I would meet him at the park. He was a good chess player. I listened to his stories, and he helped me with my sermons. Our church reached out to him, offered him a home, but Lionel said his home was with the people who needed him on the streets of Asheville. Lionel would quote to me his favorite Bible verse, Luke 4:10: 'He will put his angels in charge of you to watch over you carefully.' Lionel felt this to be his calling, to watch over his flock. His people helped build this town when they came up from Louisiana. Lionel's grandfather helped build some of these homes right here in Montford. Lionel told me he moved back here to spend his last days in the shadows of his grandfather's work. The evil that took Lionel from us can't take the memory of his good works. I look around at all these faces, all these souls that Lionel touched and made better. Just knowing Lionel made you a better person. Today we lay to rest a good man, Lionel Foret."

"Foret?" I mused out loud. His last name was Foret, French for forest. I heard Mrs. Twiggs crying as the coffin was lowered. She followed the procession, dropping a lily onto the coffin. She took a sachet from her purse. I could smell the mixture of herbs, including nettle leaves. A poultice to help Lionel rest in peace. I ran up to her to comfort her, circling around her feet, purring and rubbing up against her bare ankles. She bent down, picked me up, and hugged me. Her tears soaked my fur.

"Oh, dear, how did you ever get here?" she asked. "How did you know Lionel was here? Never mind, I'm glad to see you."

Abigail came up to us.

"Abigail, what are you doing here?" Mrs. Twiggs asked.

Abigail spoke the words I had told her earlier. "Beatrice, I hope someday Albert will say good morning back to you."

"What are you talking about?" she asked, her face turning pale white.

"Terra told me how each morning for the past ten years before opening the shop you stop and stare at your husband's photograph and say good morning."

"How could you know this? No one has ever seen me do that."

"Terra has. She's watched you every day."

Mrs. Twiggs lifted me up to her face, staring into my eyes. "Her name is Terra?"

"Yes, Terra Rowan," Abigail said. "She is a witch turned into a cat."

"Abigail, I don't know how you know these things, but I'm very worried about you." Once again, Mrs. Twiggs looked into my eyes. "If you understand me, blink once."

I blinked.

Mrs. Twiggs looked over at Abigail. "That's coincidence. It can't be possible. Why do you believe that you can understand her?"

"I don't know. I stopped trying to figure it out. At some point it makes more sense to believe the unbelievable than to deny the inevitable."

Mrs. Twiggs thought for a moment and then said, "Ask her. Ask Terra what I made for Emily the other day."

I told Abigail, who translated. "Mrs. Tangledwood was suffering from chilled bones. I guess she means arthritis. You made her a morning tea with herbs including nettle leaves and told her to take a warm bath with a lace blue agate pendant."

Mrs. Twiggs trembled like timber being felled to the ground, waving her arms madly trying to catch herself. She drew short, shallow breaths, unable to gather enough air into her lungs. She reached inside her purse and retrieved a small silver flask and took a long drink. "Are you okay?" Abigail asked, grabbing her arm and shoulder. I jumped onto her lap, purring and nuzzling.

"This can't be," Mrs. Twiggs said. "Why are you doing this to me, Abigail?"

"Terra and I need your help," Abigail said. Before she could answer, Pixel came up over emitting his nonsense noises and dropping a squirrel at our feet. "Pixel catch dinner," he said, his tail wagging. The squirrel bit Pixel's nose and took off.

"Does this cat talk too?"

"Sort of."

Mrs. Twiggs stood up and brushed off her black suit. "I think you all should come to the ladies of the Biltmore Society meeting tonight. They're going to want to meet you."

LADIES OF THE BILTMORE SOCIETY

PIXEL CLIMBED UP MRS. TWIGGS'S leg as she placed the three-tier cookie tray on the table. "Now, now, little one." Mrs. Twiggs pulled Pixel off her leg and set him on the ground. She was finalizing preparations for her club. Abigail had helped, steeping tea. I lay on the window seat, soaking up the last of the late afternoon sun. Soon the cars would pull up in front of the building, large luxury vehicles like Mercedes, BMWs and Cadillacs. Then the women would pile out. The ladies of the Biltmore Society met once a month coincidentally or not on nights of the full moon. I was anxious to be an insider to the event. I had pictured dark-hooded robes, candlelight, and whispered passwords. Truth be told, the ladies appeared in their Lilly Pulitzer, Eileen Fisher, and St. John. First Mrs. Stickman, her name suited her. She was as thin as a rail, her back slightly bent, depleted from years of calcium deficiency, her chin sharp as a chisel, her eyes sunken into her face, her hair grizzled and gray. Next came Jean Branchworthy, as wide as a sequoia trunk, her hair fire red, her moon-pie face was pleasant, but her brown eyes held a fierceness. Nupur Bartlett, a small woman of East Indian descent. I had read many books on the East Indian culture, Hindu and their religions. She was dressed not in a sari but in a tailored St. John woven linen suit. Her long, dark hair hung straight down her back. As Mrs. Bartlett took Mrs. Tangledwood's hand to help her up the front stairs, I noticed Mrs.

Tangledwood's perfectly manicured nails and a large emerald ring flashing in the sunlight. Gwendolyn Birchbark smiled kindly both at Mrs. Tangledwood and myself. She knelt down and scratched behind my ears. She had a kind face and a warm smile, a Chinese woman of elegance and refinement. Caroline Bowers was next, her freckled face was peeling from sun exposure, a gift of her Irish heritage. Wanda Raintree bore the traces of her Cherokee ancestors, including a hint of sadness in her eyes. Mrs. June Loblolly's statuesque bearing bore the traces of her supermodel past. Around her neck hung a gold chain with a Valkyrie pendant. A spry seventy, she was the youngest of the ladies. Like Biltmore Forest they represented regions from around the world drawn to this spot— just as I was. Their ceremonial hats were adorned with wreaths of fresh flowers and silver ribbons. Each unique yet similar.

Mrs. Twiggs donned her flowered hat. All the ladies gathered in the dining room at the long farmer's table and took their places, Mrs. Twiggs at the head of the table. Instead of extinguishing candles, Mrs. Twiggs dimmed the crystal chandelier. Abigail poured tea for all the ladies, eight in all, nine including Mrs. Twiggs. I wondered if it was coincidence, for nine is the number of a closed coven. In my day at that table would have sat Constance, Hester, Sarah, Rebecca, Felicity, Hannah, myself, Prudence, and at the head, Elizabeth.

Mrs. Twiggs read from a large brown leather-bound volume that was worn from use. "In 1880, George W. Vanderbilt, a young man of twenty-five, came upon the perfect spot in North Carolina's Blue Ridge Mountains for a 250-room French Renaissance chateau to be built by his friend, architect Richard Morris Hunt. The great chateau would be called Biltmore."

The ladies sipped their tea and hurrahed. Mrs. Twiggs continued reading. "Of all the majesty of the great estate, the truly outstanding achievement would be the great work of master landscaper Frederick Law Olmsted. He created a setting where Franklinia and Persian ironwood trees grow side by side with mountain laurel, rhododendron, native azaleas, and white pines. A full acre walled garden with fifty thousand tulips each spring and chrysanthemum in the autumn and of course the all-American rose garden. But Olmsted's genius didn't stop there. To confuse and impress Vanderbilt's esteemed guests, he planted secret gardens of exotic plants from around the world."

The ladies all hurrahed.

"Bamboo trees from the Orient. Baobab trees from Madagascar. Cork from the Mediterranean. Rare species of flora. Making the Biltmore a crossroads to the world," Mrs. Twiggs continued reading.

As Mrs. Twiggs spoke, I found my eyelids growing heavy. The air became thick and my breathing labored. My body screamed for sleep.

"We are at a crossroads," Elizabeth's voice echoed in my ear. We were seated at the pine table in her dining room. Candles glowed as we all watched Elizabeth in her place at the head of the table. I knew I was dreaming, but I couldn't tell if the dream world was the Leaf & Page or Elizabeth's farmhouse. Stepping between worlds I lost my foothold in reality.

Her aunt Agatha had already retired for the evening. Elizabeth's parents had not survived the brutal winter, leaving her in her aunt's care. The real cause of their death was not known to the coven—even Elizabeth questioned the circumstance. In spite of the tragedy, Elizabeth remained steadfast in her devotion to our coven. "Salem town will continue to tax the village until we are all in debtor's prison. This year the crops look to be as dismal as last. Both the townsfolk and the farmers blame witchcraft. Sitting at this table, we know differently, but to try to convince the humans would give us away." Elizabeth stood. "We must ever be on watch, careful not to reveal ourselves. I have made preparations for the harvest. There is a book of incantations that, when spoken aloud, will guarantee a good harvest. It comes with a price. This magic is neither white nor black. For that reason, I alone will be casting these spells. The book has not been opened in more than ten centuries. It wields such great power that no one witch can control it. It would take the force of a closed nine, but you're all too young, inexperienced. None of you have wanded yet. Only the Oakhaven bloodline dare try," Elizabeth said.

"Elizabeth, how will you do this on your own?" I asked.

"It's the only way," she replied. "If you're not strong enough to command the book, it will command you."

We finished our ceremony and headed to our own homes through the dark woods, carrying lanterns, the only light visible for miles. Prudence and I shared our walk, the early spring snow crunching under our feet.

"Terra, I don't like this. I don't like this at all. Elizabeth keeps too many secrets from us. We're supposed to be sisters. Her Jonathan Goodall stands to inherit not only his father's business but a tidy profit from his family's farmland holdings," Prudence whispered.

"What are you saying, Prudence?" I asked.

"I'm saying that Elizabeth stands to profit from Jonathan's good luck, and she's willing to put us all at risk for it. Why should we suffer while she profits? I deserve nice things," Prudence said.

"Elizabeth would never put a mortal before us," I disagreed with her. "She's doing this to protect us."

The glow from a lantern caught our eye. A dark, caped figure darted into Goodall and Sons Holdings on the edge of town. "Is that...?" Prudence asked me.

"Let's go take a look," I replied.

She extinguished our lantern and led me over. We peeked in the window as Elizabeth pulled down her hood. Jonathan Goodall embraced her, kissing her passionately. She returned the kiss. We watched as they spoke. "You see, you see, Terra. I told you we couldn't trust her," Prudence hissed.

"She loves him," I said, trying to pull Prudence away. "She's never hidden that fact from us. He has spoken of marriage plans."

"And what a great wedding gift to have a bumper crop of rye to build their lovely big house in town and leave us to the fields and farms."

I pulled Prudence away. "Let's go before she sees us. Let them be."

Terra sleep, Terra sleep. A small voice echoed in my head. I opened my eyes to see orange saucers an inch away from me, and then a white-covered paw biffed me in the head. "Pixel play. You it," he said before running off at a frantic pace through the ladies' legs.

"Now we come to why I have called this special meeting of the Biltmore Society," Mrs. Twiggs said. "The founder of our society, Olmsted, believed there was more to this world than meets the eye. Traveling the world in search of exotic flora and fauna, he came across cultures that believed there are powers that walk among us. He found such a culture here in Asheville. The settlers of the Appalachian Mountains believe there are forces of nature that can be controlled. Olmsted studied the local folklore. He believed as they did that the trees and rivers and mountains had their own spiritual identity. That even the creatures of the mountains have a soul." Before I could agree with her, Mrs. Twiggs picked me up and continued speaking. "This gray tabby has been coming to my store for ten years. She taps on the door and follows me about my day's activities. I've always felt a connection to her and didn't understand why. She looks at me as though she understands what I am saying to her, and she does. Today I found out that she can communicate with us."

Emma stood up. She took a sniff of her teacup. "Beatrice, what exactly is in this tea tonight?" And then she turned to me and looked deep into my eyes as though, if just for a brief moment, she believed I could talk.

"Emma Tangledwood, what are you implying?" Mrs. Twiggs put her hands on her wide hips. The rest of the women became quiet. "Mrs. Bowers, Jean Branchworthy, not for a moment do you believe I'm crazy? Doris Stickman, how many years have I known you?" Mrs. Twiggs asked.

"Stickman, Branchworthy, Emma Tangledwood." Hearing the names together, I finally understood. "The ladies of the Biltmore Society are a coven of Wiccans." I leapt out of Mrs. Twiggs's arms and pulled Abigail out of the dining room into the kitchen.

"What are you doing, Terra? She was about to ask me to explain," Abigail said.

"You can't say anything, Abigail," I told her, arching my back and pacing along the counter.

"What are you talking about, Terra? We need her help."

"These women are all Wiccans."

"It's just a bunch of old women having tea, telling stories," Abigail said.

"It's their last names. Tangledwood, Stickman, Mrs. Twiggs, those are all parts of trees."

"You're not making any sense," Abigail said.

"Witches' true names date back to the times of the Druids who held trees sacred. The word Druid translates to keepers of the oaks. These names date back to the very beginning of time. They change throughout the millennia from the Druid name for oak to oak haven and many derivatives, but they all have the witches' spirit tree in their name. As I told you, mine is Rowan, which means mountain ash. Elizabeth, the leader of my coven, her last name was Oakhaven. Her descendants stretch back to the old ones."

"So what is a Wiccan?" Abigail asked.

"Wiccans, true Wiccans—not the religious version of nature worshippers they've become in your time—but the real Wiccans have bloodlines that date back to witches. When a witch marries a mortal, they have to give up their powers, but their bloodline continues through their children. Their blood is mixed with mortal blood making them a half witch or Wiccan. There are exceptions; they're very rare. That bloodline continues as the centuries pass. Without training, the Wiccans lose their power and don't even know that they carry the bloodline. These women all have powers they are not aware of."

"What's the problem? Tell them. They can help us too," Abigail said, making it sound so easy.

"You don't understand. Besides Mrs. Twiggs and Mrs. Tangledwood, I don't know these other women. Their bloodlines could hold white or black magic. I could unleash evil into the world. We must tread carefully and learn their real purpose," I told her.

"What do you want me to do?"

"Abigail, will you please come in here, right now, dear?" Mrs. Twiggs called from the dining room. "This is Abigail. She can hear the cat talk. Abigail, talk to the cat," Mrs. Twiggs commanded.

Abigail stood silent, assessing the room and the waiting ladies. "Mrs. Twiggs, I don't know what you want me to do."

"Abigail, at the funeral today, what about all those things you told me that no one but the cat could have known?" Mrs. Twiggs gave me a shocked look.

"Mrs. Twiggs, you were very upset. It's very understandable. A friend of yours was murdered in your alley. No one would expect you not to be upset," Abigail said.

Mrs. Stickman cleared her throat and stood. "Beatrice, we're going to call an end to the meeting."

"Wait, don't go," Mrs. Twiggs pleaded.

Shaking their heads, the ladies filed out, one after another, leaving Mrs. Twiggs alone with Abigail and myself. Mrs. Twiggs walked over and locked the front door, then turned to us with a stern look. "What's this all about, Abigail?"

Abigail explained everything I had told her about the ladies. Mrs. Twiggs plopped down on a tiny wooden chair that creaked and wobbled, not wanting to accept the load. "Is the cat speaking to you now?"

"Tell Mrs. Twiggs I can help her make a potion that will unleash her powers. If she is a true Wiccan, she will be able to understand me," I said.

Abigail explained to Mrs. Twiggs. I jumped up on the dining room table and rubbed up against her, staring into her eyes and blinking. She rubbed my head. "I understand, Terra." The three of us worked late into the night, grinding various herbs and plants. "Terra, no eye of newt or bat wing?" Abigail asked with a sarcastic air.

"If you have some, that would be great, but it won't help."

As we concocted the potion, Mrs. Twiggs took notes in her leather-bound book. I glanced over her shoulder as she flipped pages. There were scribblings of other potions and cures. I asked Abigail to ask her about them. "These are some of the 'receipts' as the mountain folk call them. They have been handed down over the years. I've collected them as I travel through the mountains, talking to the locals. Some of these receipts are from Europe. This one is for nosebleeds. You hold a knife up and let the blood drip on to the edge of the blade. It cuts the nosebleed."

"Ask her about these drawings," I said.

Abigail relayed the question. "Some of the original settlers in the Appalachians came from Ireland. These are some of the gravestone markings I found near Pisgah Forest. I believe they are Ogham, a Celtic alphabet," Mrs. Twiggs explained. "The letters are arranged in different orders to bring forth different spells. On headstones, they were used to help the dead cross over from one world to another."

I glanced at Abigail, nodding in agreement and then told them, "The Ogham alphabet was used by the Druids. Many of the written incantations Elizabeth showed us were written in Ogham. My spirit tree, the ash, is a vertical line with five horizontal lines branching out to the right."

Mrs. Twiggs flipped the page. I saw the symbols for the ash, the oak, and the thorn. "These three are the symbols of what the Appalachians called the magic trinity. I found these drawings on

Black Mountain."

"Agatha Hollows," I said.

Abigail looked at me. She knew of whom I spoke.

"Pixel tired." Pixel came and flopped on the dining room table, rolled on his back once and then laid on his side. His eyes closed slowly, his tail slapping against the wood, his front paws kneading the air as though it were a feather pillow.

When the potion was finished, Abigail and Mrs. Twiggs looked at me. Abigail said, "Do we say something now? Hocus-pocus. Abracadabra."

"You can if you want, but it won't do any good. Mrs. Twiggs just needs to drink it. If she's a Wiccan, the potion will enter her bloodstream and open up her bloodline. Her blood knowledge is encrypted into her DNA. Think of it like an adrenaline shot to wake up her sleeping nucleotide."

Abigail gave me a confused glance.

"I've been reading every book on genetics I could find for three hundred years to find a way to turn back into my true self," I said.

On Abigail's direction, Mrs. Twiggs drank the potion. Pixel opened his eyes and reached a lazy paw toward the empty cookie tray. We sat and waited. Mrs. Twiggs cleared her throat. "I don't feel anything."

I knew it didn't work because Mrs. Twiggs's aura color did not change. It was sky blue, a beautiful color for a pure heart and old soul, but Wiccans have two aura colors. Mrs. Twiggs looked at me. "It didn't work, did it, Terra?"

I blinked twice for no.

"I'd like to try it," a voice from the sitting room chimed in. We stared with surprise; we thought everyone else had left. Out from the dark corner, Mrs. Tangledwood stood, her gnarled hands reaching for the glass. She downed the potion before any of us could stop her. Within seconds, her back straightened, she dropped her cane, her white hair turned raven black, her milky eyes became clear blue sapphires, her aura color turned from gray to forest green and yellow.

"Emma," Beatrice exclaimed. "What is happening?"

"I can see." She did a short jig and danced around the table. Pixel jumped off the table and joined her.

"Emma, your hip, your bad knee?"

"I don't feel a thing, Beatrice. I feel wonderful, better than I have in years."

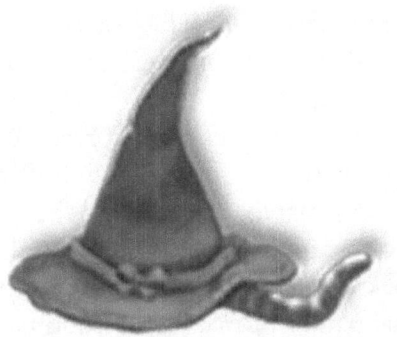

THE PUMPKIN FESTIVAL

THE SUN SHONE BRIGHTLY OVER the garden at the Biltmore Estate. Pumpkins brought in from the local farmers lay across the wide green lawn. Mrs. Tangledwood dashed between the rows of stacked gourds like a Russian ballerina. Her turning had set her biological clock back at least twenty years. It was the most remarkable turn I had ever seen. "Emma, what have you done to your hair?" Mrs. Stickwood asked her.

"Do you like it?" Mrs. Tangledwood asked, reaching up and touching her now raven-black curls.

"And your skin looks so smooth."

"Yes, doesn't it?"

"And where's your cane?"

"Caroline, it's the most remarkable thing." As Mrs. Tangledwood spoke, I hissed at her, warning her not to reveal her secret. It was too soon for the others to know. For now she appeared to the others as Mrs. Tangledwood, but as her powers grew, she would continue to look younger.

Abigail unloaded the last of the pumpkins while Pixel rounded up field mice. Seeing Pixel sitting next to a pumpkin surrounded by mice made me think of the animated movie *Cinderella*. No pumpkins would turn into carriages tonight, but there was definitely magic in the air. I could feel it swirling across the field, stirring in the trees like the last of the fall leaves floating to the ground, crunching underfoot. The rest of the Biltmore Society ladies arrived. To my horror, they were dressed like witches or what they thought witches should dress like, black cloaks, warts on noses and green face paint. They carried broomsticks and wore the pointed hats that were considered witch hats. Abigail stared at me . I shook my head.

I shrugged, at least the hats were correct. When a young witch wands, she is given such a hat that symbolizes the pyramid. The earth walkers, white witches, instructed the pharaohs on the construction of the pyramids, using the universal truth equation. The triangle. Ash, oak and thorn bind all the powers of the universe to form the eternal trinity of man, witch, and nature. Yes, the hats are correct, but I wouldn't try flying on the brooms.

Mrs. Tangledwood greeted them. "You ladies look wonderful. I've assigned each of you a task. Mrs. Stickman and I will handle pumpkin sales, Mrs. Branchworthy will oversee concessions, Mrs. Bowers, you're in charge of the haunted hayride, and you, Beatrice, will handle the hay bale maze. Let's make this a great day."

Abigail and I followed Mrs. Twiggs to the right corner of the field where the volunteers were finishing construction of the hay bale maze. Over a thousand bales had been donated by local farms along with homemade scarecrows made by the 4-H Club. "Aren't you going to change into your witch costume like the rest of the ladies?" Abigail asked.

"Oh, no, dear, I don't feel right after what happened to Mrs. Tangledwood. I don't want to tempt the fates," she replied.

"Oh," Abigail said. "How can I help? How does this whole thing work?"

Mrs. Twiggs pulled a folded piece of paper from her coat pocket. She unfolded it and placed it on a hay bale. "This is the plan for the maze. There's only one way in but several ways to return."

I jumped up next to the map and studied the hand-drawn sketch. It was quite detailed.

"Abigail, I can collect tickets. Do you want to see if one of the other ladies needs help?" Mrs. Twiggs asked.

Abigail nodded. We took off, stopping at the concession stand for a fresh cider donut. "Mmmm, good," Pixel said, climbing up Abigail's leg for another bite. He had a sixth sense when it came to food. He appeared out of nowhere after we reached the donut stand. Surveying the grounds, I saw the crowds filtering in, many children wearing Halloween costumes. The sound of laughter trailed behind us as we reached the woods where families boarded the horse cart for the hayride.

I nuzzled up against the cart horse. He whinnied and lowered his head so I could rub against him. I had a special fondness for horses both as a young witch and as a cat. Mrs. Bowers sat on a bale of hay, accepting tickets as one of the volunteers helped customers into the cart. Holding the reins, the handsome young man fixed his gaze on Abigail. She pulled the collar of her leather jacket around her neck to hide her blush. She might be used to such looks but did not take comfort from them. Just the opposite. I nudged her toward the cart. The young man reached down his hand from his seat. "Hi, I'm Bryson. Do you want a ride?"

I pushed my head against Abigail who grabbed his hand and jumped up. She settled next to him. I sat next to Abigail. Pixel tumbled up, balancing next to me. Bryson jerked the reins, and we took off down the trail through the tunnel of trees, leading into Biltmore Forest. Makeshift ghosts and skeletons hung from trees, swaying in the breeze. A speaker hidden by shrubs played eerie music and scary laughter. "You never told me your name?" Bryson asked.

"It's Abigail." She smiled shyly, glancing down.

"I don't recognize you from 4-H. Are you new?"

"I'm new to town."

"Oh. Where are you from? Visiting? Vacationing? Doing the world tour of pumpkin fests?" He grinned.

"I'm just passing through," Abigail said, shifting farther away on the seat.

Bryson thought for a moment. "If you're still around in an hour, would you want to walk around the fest? Maybe get some cider?"

Abigail turned silent. I could see she was troubled by his affection. As we rode deeper into the woods, bouncing with every bump, giggles came up from behind us. Zombies appeared, approached us, and the kids in the back of the cart screamed. Abigail clung to Bryson. Pixel growled. Bryson put his arm around Abigail, smiling. I knew she was safe with him. He was a watcher. I had spotted him earlier in the day. His aura light was the same as Lionel's, strong and pure. I saw him watch over the children as he helped them climb into the cart. Know it or not, Bryson was here to watch over Abigail.

The trail reached its apex and began its curve back toward the festival grounds. As we turned the corner, ghosts appeared from behind the trees. These were not volunteers, and none of the riders saw them. I thought it ironic to have a haunted hayride in an actual haunted wood. Thankfully I alone could see the ghosts that clung to the Biltmore Estate, some workers killed during construction, others taken by illness. They watched peacefully as we trotted by. They were harmless souls. Abigail wiggled out from under Bryson's arm as we returned to the open field. Happy hay riders jumped off the cart, giggling and moving on to the next activity. "Can we meet up?" Bryson asked.

Abigail grabbed Bryson's phone from his pocket, typed something in before handing it back. "Call me sometime," she said, hopping off the buckboard. I looked behind watching Bryson watching Abigail walk away. We spent the rest of the afternoon exploring the grounds and checking in with the Society ladies. We found Mrs. Tangledwood, wandering around the tables of the local jewelry artists. Abigail picked up a copper bracelet. After checking the price tag, she returned it. Mrs. Tangledwood was admiring herself in a tabletop mirror. She was trying on a silver chain that held a dangling large almost emerald-green stone. She turned to Abigail. "What do you think? It's simple but elegant." She said.

"Is that an emerald?" Abigail asked.

"Oh, no, it's hiddenite."

"Hiddenite?"

"Yes, it's only found in Hiddenite, North Carolina. Hiddenite is not that far from here, and the gem is more rare than emeralds. William Earl Hidden, who was in the area searching for plutonium for Thomas Edison, discovered it. Wearing hiddenite is supposed to encourage growth," Mrs. Tangledwood said, fingering the stone. "That's it. I've decided. I'm going to take it. After all, why shouldn't I have nice things?" She negotiated a price with the jeweler.

When the sun was low in the sky, we returned to Mrs. Twiggs. On reaching the maze, Mrs. Twiggs was collecting tickets from the last customers.

"Oh, Abigail dear, I'm glad you're back. Would you mind taking my place for a few minutes? This is the last group."

"Sure, Mrs. Twiggs." Abigail sat on the hay bale. Mrs. Twiggs hurried off toward the concession stand. Out of the corner of my eye, I saw a mouse scamper by, Pixel hot after it. I couldn't resist the chase. I flew after Pixel and his prey. I lost track of time, my mind fixating on the mouse. My body betrays me or something confuses me. Why did I leave Abigail alone? I hurried back to the maze. She was gone.

I circled around the perimeter, calling to her. I climbed over a ten-foot wall of hay, searching for her. I saw movement in the heart of the maze, a wall shifting, closing in and then another and then another. I leapt to the ground and ran through the maze as walls closed in behind me, screaming out to Abigail. I could hear her screams muffled by the bales. I followed her voice until I reached the center of the maze where Abigail lay on the ground staring up at a scarecrow, its eyes glowing bright red as it leapt off its post. I stood in front of it, trying to block it from reaching Abigail. "Run, Abigail, run," I commanded as I leapt onto the scarecrow and tore at its eyes, pulling out its stuffing. It fell to pieces around me. But then all the pieces came to life, crawling along the ground like thousands of spiders until they came together to form the creature again.

Off in the distance, Abigail screamed, and then she became silent. I ran from the scarecrow to find Bryson holding her in his arms. Abigail was hysterical, tears streaming down her face.

"Are you okay? Abigail, are you okay?" he asked her, keeping her close.

She caught a breath. "I—"

"You were lost. It's easy to get lost in here. It's dark, it's big. It's okay." Bryson said, putting his arm around her shoulder.

"But—" Abigail said.

Bryson took her hand. "Let me lead you out."

Abigail nodded. I followed them out of the maze, giving one last glance toward the scarecrow that was back up on his post, his eyes dull buttons.

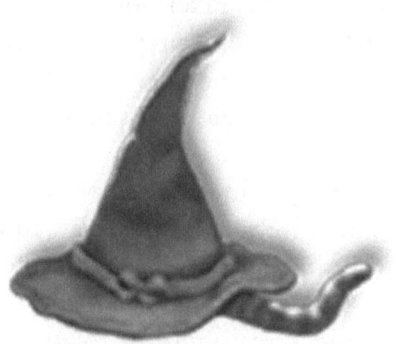

LET IT BLEED

I WATCHED ABIGAIL AS SHE WANDERED around the vintage vinyl shop with Bryson, their shoulders touched as they flipped through the albums. Bryson gave her a crooked smile, glancing at her from the corner of his eye. He picked up an album. I sat quietly by the headphone rack where two young girls sat listening to tracks. I could hear Stevie Nicks through the headphones, singing "Rhiannon." As always no one paid attention to me. I walked confidently, wanting to appear as if I belonged in the store. I listened in on their conversation, grateful Bryson was Abigail's watcher.

"I'm so glad you called me." He held up a Partridge Family album. "My Partridge Family collection was running dangerously low." He smiled.

Abigail returned the smile. "About yesterday and the maze… I let my imagination run wild. I think I was scared because I was lost in there."

"No worries." He picked up "Let it Bleed" by the Rolling Stones. "Have you ever heard this? This is a classic." He took Abigail by the hand and walked her over to the listening station. He carefully took the album out of the cover and placed it on the phonograph. Then he crouched down and placed the stylus in the groove.

Abigail put the headphones on and started bobbing her head. I could hear the opening guitar strains of "Gimme Shelter." Bryson tapped his foot along to Charlie Watts. Abigail's smile disappeared; her eyes grew wide. She tore the headphones off and ran out from the store.

After chasing her to where she collapsed in an alleyway, I rubbed against her and asked, "Abigail, what is it? What's wrong?"

"Gimme Shelter. That song." Abigail paused, running her hands through her hair. "Terra, my parents were killed during Katrina. My mother was singing that song to us as we huddled on the roof of our house. I watched waters drag them away from me, my mother screaming my name as her hands reached out for me. All I can remember of her is that song and the fear in her eyes not for herself, but for her five-year-old daughter. She stuffed the pocket watch in my backpack. She told me it was a family heirloom. I have to get that watch back from the pawnshop." Abigail paused. "My adopted parents never told me." She rubbed her arm, scratching at her tattoo, then she knelt down and picked me up, cradling me. I rubbed my head softly against her hand, purring. I felt her five-year-old child crying. "I can see their faces, Terra. It's their voices in my head."

Bryson appeared in the alley. "Abigail, what's wrong?"

Abigail hugged him and kissed his cheek. "I'm sorry, Bryson, that song brought back some bad memories, and I kind of freaked out."

"I knew I should have played the Partridge Family instead." Bryson laughed. Abigail smiled through her tears. "Are you hungry? How do you feel about Chinese?"

Abigail looked up into his eyes and nodded her head. They walked down the narrow cobblestone sidewalk to the Noodle Shop. It was unusually warm for an October day. Most of the patio tables were filled. Bryson whispered something to the young waiter. He was adorned with tattoo symbols and short dreadlocks. His soul patch was dyed red, his T-shirt read, "One World, One Love." He led them to a corner table overlooking the town square. I jumped up onto a chair next to Abigail against the wall hidden from view from the other customers. Bryson glanced down at me and smiled. He had not asked Abigail once, "what's with the cat?" His watcher's intuition told him I was watching Abigail, and that was enough for him to accept me.

After they poured the tea, Abigail asked, " So were you born here?"

Bryson peered over the menu at her. "Actually I was born in

Fletcher. It's about fifteen minutes south of here. My family breeds horses."

Abigail smiled. "Horses, that's nice."

The hipster waiter came over and took their order. He stared at me once and then at Bryson before walking away. A short while later, he returned with shumai dumplings stuffed with shrimp and chicken. Bryson grabbed his chopsticks, picked up the dumpling, and dunked it in the sauce. Abigail fumbled with her sticks, dropping her dumpling several times. She looked up in frustration. Bryson smiled, lifted a dumpling up with his stick, dipped it and held it up for her. She took a bite and smiled. "It takes some time to get used to these things."

Abigail picked up a fork and stabbed another dumpling. "How'd you find me in the maze?"

"What's that?" he asked, finishing his third dumpling.

"The maze, you just showed up."

"I was walking past, and I heard screams."

I could tell Abigail didn't quite believe his answer. The festival was noisy. It would be very hard to hear any sounds behind hundreds of bales of hay. Lionel knew he was a watcher and that he had a purpose. It was in his bloodline, but Bryson was very young. I could tell he didn't quite understand what drew him to Abigail besides the fact she was a beautiful young girl.

Bryson sipped his tea. "I don't know anything about you, Abigail."

"Not much to tell. I'm from Chicago. At least that's where my adoptive parents raised me."

"What are you doing in Asheville?"

Abigail put her fork down. "I don't know. I honestly don't know, Bryson."

"There's a band playing at the Orange Peel tonight. Friends of mine are roadies. If you think you might want to hang out, it's all ages."

Abigail smiled. "Yeah, I could use some normal in my life right now. That'd be cool."

"How about I meet you outside at nine?" Bryson smiled back.

"Cool. See you then."

The waiter brought the check. Bryson grabbed it quickly. "It's on me."

As they spoke, I looked over Bryson's shoulder to the young woman sitting on the sidewalk bench in front of the tiny restaurant. She appeared out of place among the other young people, dressed in tattered jeans and cardigan sweaters, walking up and down Pack Square. She pulled a pocket watch from her frock, clicked it open as though to show me the time. Then she turned her head. I could see that half her face was burned away. The fur on my back stood up.

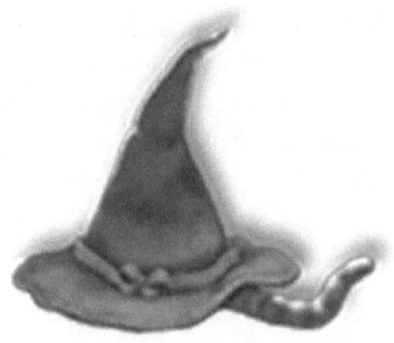

TRANSFIXATION

I STOOD OUTSIDE THE ORANGE PEEL with Abigail, who was shivering in the late fall evening air. The line grew longer as the hour grew later. There was no sign of Bryson. Abigail checked her phone. No message. She shook her leg impatiently, twisting her head left and right, standing on tiptoes to look over the crowd. I meandered through her legs to calm her. Patience was not her virtue. After an hour or so, the line disappeared into the building. We could hear the opening band. Abigail leaned against the brick wall. "I don't understand, Terra, this was his idea. Why would he blow me off?"

I did not think for a moment that Bryson stood her up on purpose. I could tell from the moment he saw her at the pumpkin fest that his life was intertwined with hers. I watched him watch her and knew almost nothing would keep him from seeing her tonight. I did not relay my worry to her. Abigail is a strong young woman, but her strength would be tested. "Let's go, Terra, I'm tired of waiting."

Abigail pulled her collar up and headed at a steady pace down the crowded street.

We arrived at Mrs. Twiggs's as she was getting ready for bed. She was gracious enough to allow Abigail and I to stay in a small room in the back of the shop. I felt safe at the Leaf & Page. The spirits that lingered there were kind and well meaning.

"You're back earlier than I thought," Mrs. Twiggs said. "How was the concert?"

"Bryson never showed."

"Oh dear, I'm sorry. He seemed like such a nice boy."

"Yeah, I thought so," Abigail said, taking off her boots and jacket and leaving them by the front door.

"Let me fix you some tea." Mrs. Twiggs bustled toward the kitchen. We followed her.

I ran over to the fireplace where Pixel was sound asleep on his back, all four paws in the air. "Me hungry," he murmured in his sleep.

Abigail sat in the leather wing-back chair, rubbing her eyes with her hands. I leapt into her lap.

"Abigail, is that the only memory you have of your biological parents? The hurricane?" I asked.

"What? What'd you say, Terra?" Abigail asked, stroking my fur absentmindedly.

"You said the song 'Gimme Shelter' triggered that memory of the night you lost your parents."

"I don't know, Terra, I've heard 'Gimme Shelter' hundreds of times. I like the Stones. I don't know why I remembered this time. I was holding Bryson's hand and I felt, I don't know, safe? And then it came to me."

"Abigail, I'd like to try something with you tonight if you trust me."

"What are you talking about?"

"Let me explain. Sometimes when you try to remember the simplest thing whether it's a grocery list or the title of a book you read recently, it seems to slip your mind. The harder you try to remember the harder it is to pull back that memory."

"I still don't understand what you're talking about," Abigail said, furrowing her brow in confusion.

"If you stop trying to retrieve that memory, sometimes it comes back by itself. By searching for it, you expend all your energy, you run down thousands of paths along your brain synapses. Think of it as RAM memory, limited. If you reach capacity Googling your memory, your processor locks up. You concentrate more on the process of trying to retrieve the memory than letting the memory appear. I'd like you to relax and clear your mind. Don't think about anything. A clean slate."

Mrs. Twiggs appeared, holding a sliver tea service. "What are you two up to?" she asked seeing me staring eye to eye with Abigail. Pixel stirred at the sound of the rattling cookie tray and ran over to wind through Mrs. Twiggs's feet, meowing softly.

"Terra wants me to clear my mind so I can retrieve some childhood memories."

Mrs. Twiggs sat in the opposing chair. "Like hypnosis?" she asked, pouring the tea.

Abigail shrugged.

"What type of childhood memories?" Mrs. Twiggs asked, handing her a cup with a ladyfinger dangling off the saucer. Pixel lifted his paw and reached for the delicate cookie.

"Nothing I really want to talk about," Abigail said.

"Oh dear, I see." Mrs. Twiggs thought for a moment. "Sometimes it's better to face your demons. Bring them out into the light."

I jerked my head back and stared at Mrs. Twiggs. There was more to her than I had yet realized. She understood that some shadow was blocking Abigail's memories. Whether it was a Freudian self-defense mechanism or something much more malignant, I wanted to draw back the curtain. "What do you need me to do, Terra?" Abigail asked.

"Close your eyes and clear your mind." I watched the moving pictures in Abigail's head, events from this evening, the Chinese restaurant, and the pumpkin fest. She avoided thinking about the scarecrow. I could hear her heartbeat and breathing slow. I sang softly to her. Elizabeth had taught me the ancient art of transfixation, the ability to direct one's thoughts down the pathways of your mind and to carry others with you. Elizabeth would come to me in my dreams by this means, and we would converse in secret. This was the first time I ever tried this ability with anyone save Elizabeth. Elizabeth told me it began with the succession of high-pitched sounds. Pixel yowled softly before turning over and falling back to sleep. Like a safecracker clicking the tumblers slowly waiting to hear the catch of each gear, I listened for the right notes to open Abigail's stored memories. These notes drew the listener in until two minds became one. I sang those notes softly to Abigail, who followed me down the path until we were standing face-to-face not as cat to human but as my true self, seventeen-year-old Terra Rowan, the young witch of Salem. Abigail smiled widely and hugged me. "Terra, this is you. This is who you are."

"Yes, Abigail. This is me."

Abigail glanced around us. We were floating in a white mist. "Where are we? What's happening?"

"This is what Elizabeth called clarity, the birthplace of all your thoughts." As I spoke, the white mist turned pale gray.

"What's happening, Terra?"

"You're scared, Abigail. You don't want to see the truth." Lightning struck in the distance, and the pale gray mist turned ashy black.

"Terra, I can't do this."

I took both her hands in mine. "Just follow me. Just follow me, Abigail." As my words came out, I could feel her hands slipping from my grasp. She began floating away.

"Terra," she screamed. Her voice echoing as she distanced away from me. I could not hold her. The hurricane was coming. She was gone. Her eyes flew open.

Mrs. Twiggs grabbed her hand. "Darling, you're sweaty and breathing heavy. What's going on?"

Abigail caught her breath. She shook her head, stood up and stretched. "Nothing. I'm going to bed. I'm tired."

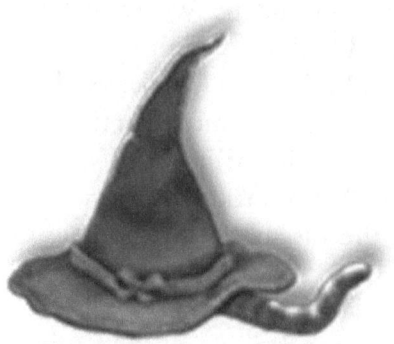

ME FAMILIAR

WE ARRIVED HOME AS THE sun rose over the mountain. Mist covered the ground. We were weary. Pixel was draped over Abigail's shoulder. In the foggy distance, I could make out the pale blue eyes of our tracker. The bacon was gone from our porch. He had left a present, a bundle of mountain ash sticks, rowan—he knew my name.

Soon we sat on the porch, Abigail sipping her tea as I wrestled with Pixel. As hard as I fought my cat tendencies, they still managed to overtake me. Abigail watched intensely. "If you're a witch, why can't you use your powers to change yourself back?" Abigail asked me.

"It doesn't work like that, Abigail," I said, flipping Pixel onto his back. "The spell that turned me was cast from another witch, a very powerful witch, Elizabeth Oakhaven, the leader of our coven. And only she can break the spell," I said.

"Why hasn't she done that?"

"Elizabeth was killed during the Salem witch trials. All of my coven were tried and convicted and put to death." I shuddered recalling the moment when Elizabeth's neck snapped on the gallows.

"That's why she turned you into a cat? To save you from the trials?"

I stared at her.

"I see," Abigail said.

"Someone betrayed us. They told our secret. They took my sisters' lives, my life and my future."

Pixel flew back and forth across the porch, emitting loud noises. "Tracker, Tracker." I had to hold back my instinct to chase him. "Pixel, quiet. I smell him too. It's okay." Pixel settled down.

"Terra, something Mrs. Twiggs said at the Biltmore Society meeting has bothered me," Abigail said in a musing tone. "She said that Asheville was the crossroads to the world. The same word that the voices in my head have been saying since I turned thirteen."

I jumped onto Abigail's lap to reveal the next part of the puzzle. "Lionel thought Asheville was his crossroad and I, too, was drawn here by some magic."

"Why am I here, Terra? Why did I meet you? Why am I the only one who can understand you?"

"I don't know. Only a witch or a turned Wiccan would be able to understand me in my current state."

"I don't feel like a witch."

"What do you think witches feel like?" I asked sarcastically.

"You know—I twitch my nose but nothing happens, I blink my eyes—same nothing. When I was sweeping the cabin, I didn't feel an urge to climb on top of the broom."

I laughed. "Abigail, it's not that easy. I have not met a witch in three hundred years. There is something special about you, but I would know if you were a witch."

"How does Lionel play a part in all this?" Abigail asked, settling back onto the porch step.

"That eludes me for now. There are different planes of magic in this world and others. Even mortals have unlocked magic without realizing it. Elizabeth told me of some humans who are called watchers. What we would call the human version of a familiar."

"Like Pixel." Pixel lifted his head. "Me Terra familiar."

I thought for a moment, tilted my head, and realized he was right. "Pixel, I haven't quite thought of it that way, but you might just be," I said to him.

"Me familiar, me familiar," Pixel chanted, prancing around the deck like he was royalty. His tail straight up in the air with his head turning left to right.

"Elizabeth's familiar was a wolf. I never wanded, so I was never given a familiar." My thoughts returned to Lionel. Human watchers knowingly or not protect white witches. I believe Lionel was such a watcher. He didn't know I was a witch, but something inside him—maybe magic or kindness or the angels he sang of—made him keep watch over me and the other street folk."

"The voices are getting stronger in my head," Abigail said.

Abigail reached into the cooler that Mrs. Twiggs had packed for us full of vegetables from her garden, cheese and a mason jar of Mrs. Twiggs's moonshine. Tea wasn't the only refreshment served to the ladies at the Biltmore Society meetings. Abigail took a sip and shuddered. Pixel stood on Abigail's lap to give it a sniff. His little sandpaper tongue slurped up a taste. "Me like, me like." He stuck his head down and gulped it down before Abigail could pull it away from him. "Me like," Pixel said, walking wobbly down the stairs of the porch, collapsing at the bottom, rolling back and forth on his back. "Pixel, sleepy."

Abigail stepped off the porch, picked Pixel up, and carried him sideways into the cabin. Pixel purred loudly, and then he bit her arm. They settled onto the cot, and both fell asleep. I watched them for a few moments before leaving, and then I went back down into town to visit Reverend Stillwater's church.

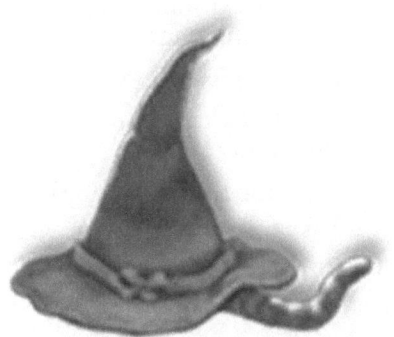

FIRST BAPTIST CHURCH

THE FIRST BAPTIST CHURCH OF Montford was built in the 1880s under the careful eye of Richard Sharpe Smith, the architect of the Biltmore house. Constructed from limestone left over from the Biltmore Estate, it started as a small wooden church for freed slaves who originally settled on the grounds of what would become the estate. George Vanderbilt purchased the land from the pastor and the congregation with a promise to rebuild their church in the Montford area just outside downtown Asheville. Lionel's great-grandfather was one of the freed slaves who helped build the new church, stone by stone. Lionel would take me there and touch the limestone. He said it had healing properties and gave him the ability to reach into the past to touch his great-grandfather whom he had never met. I stared at the cornerstone, missing Lionel.

Reverend Stillwater's family had traveled the Louisiana yellow fever trail in the 1880s from the same parish Lionel's family had come from. Lionel had told me that is why he felt a connection to Reverend Stillwater. I hoped I might find something in the parish records about Lionel's bloodlines. Somewhere in Lionel's past was magic, and that magic brought about his death, I feared.

I crawled my way through the broken basement window and up to the reverend's office. He was there with the two detectives who had questioned Abigail. They were now questioning the reverend. I slinked into a corner and listened.

"Reverend Stillwater, you say you saw Lionel the night of his murder?"

"Yes, that's correct. Lionel stopped in early evening. I'd say maybe five o'clock before heading to the park. That's not so unusual. He would stop by often." The reverend sat forward in his chair, clasping his hands on the old oak desk.

"What did you talk about?"

"Lionel was troubled for the past couple of weeks. His dreams were troubled. You have to understand I care for a lot of the homeless. Many end up on the streets because of mental illness, but I don't believe that was the case with Lionel."

"What about these dreams?"

"Lionel told me he had a recurring dream of a young girl in trouble. The dream ended the same way with the girl hanging by her neck from an oak tree," the reverend said.

"I see," the young detective said, scratching notes in his pad. "Do you know of anyone who would want to hurt Lionel?"

After pausing for a minute, the reverend shook his head. "Not at all. Everyone loved Lionel. You asked me all this already. Why are you really here?"

The young detective reached into his pocket and pulled out a photograph. He handed it to the reverend. "Do you know this man?"

The reverend stared at the picture. "He looks like a kid."

"Seventeen years old. His name was Bryson Wald."

The reverend shook his head.

The detective took back the photograph. "He was killed at three a.m. this morning, the exact same time of death as Lionel and with what we believe was the same knife, a silver knife."

"That's terrible. Did you say three a.m.?"

"Yes, according to the coroner."

The reverend scratched his beard and then said, "That's the witching hour."

"What do you mean?"

"Christ died at three p.m. The witching hour is directly opposite at three a.m." The reverend paused.

"We'd like you to speak to the congregation and ask the homeless you work with. Anyone who might have known Lionel or Bryson," the detective said, standing up. "We'll have extra patrol in the area. One last thing." He pulled a piece of paper out of his pocket and placed it in front of the reverend. I could see it was a copy of Abigail's driver's license. "Do you know this girl?"

The reverend shook his head.

"She's homeless, been sleeping in her car. We found her name and phone number in Bryson's phone."

He looked at it again. "I have seen her. She was at Lionel's funeral talking to Mrs. Twiggs." The reverend paused before continuing. "Do you think she had something to do with the murders?"

"For now she's a person of interest but call immediately if you see or hear anything of her whereabouts."

The reverend took the detective's card and nodded in agreement.

After the police officers left, Reverend Stillwater grabbed his Bible. I heard him reading the passage he read over Lionel's funeral about the angels. I knew angels couldn't protect us. They hadn't protected us in Salem.

There are several ways to kill a witch. The Salem witch hunters were wrong about some. Drowning or hanging won't kill a witch; they will only send her powers into a new vessel. Fire or silver through the heart will extinguish their life force. Whoever killed Lionel and Bryson knew, however, that both men were protected by magic and that they were watching over Abigail. If I am to save her, I must find out who killed them and why they want Abigail. For now, I needed to warn Abigail that the police were looking for her.

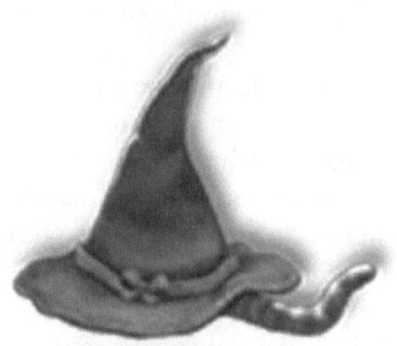

DARK VOICES

I RAN BACK TO THE LEAF & Page as quickly as my four little furry paws would advance me, but I was too late. As I turned the corner, I saw the two detectives dragging a handcuffed Abigail out of the shop. She was kicking and screaming. Pixel was clawing at one of the detective's legs and hissing. He shook him off, causing Pixel to tumble down the crooked walk and crash into a garbage can. Mrs. Twiggs came out of the store, sobbing. "Wait, this is wrong. She had nothing to do with Lionel's death."

The detective ignored Mrs. Twiggs, who put her arms around Abigail. "I'll call my attorney. We'll post bail."

Abigail nodded her head and climbed into the back of the sedan. I ran up to her window. "Abigail, we'll come for you. We will come for you," I called to her. The car took off.

Mrs. Twiggs bent down and picked me up. Pixel ran up to her. She scooped him up also and hugged us both tightly. "I wish I could understand you," she said, staring deep into my eyes. "Emma. We must get Emma." Mrs. Twiggs carried us into the store and called Mrs. Tangledwood.

A short while later, a smoky quartz Bentley pulled up in front of the Leaf & Page, its window sticker still affixed to the passenger window. Mrs. Tangledwood leapt out of the car and flung open the front door.

"Beatrice, this is outrageous. I've contacted my attorney. He's meeting us at the police station."

"Mrs. Tangledwood," I said. "Abigail is not safe. We have to bring her home."

Mrs. Tangledwood lifted me up. "Then let's make that happen, shall we?"

Mrs. Twiggs grabbed her purple velvet coat and locked up the store. Pixel and I leapt into the back seat of the Bentley. When we arrived at the police station, I climbed into Mrs. Tangledwood's Hermes Birkin bag. She peeked in at me. "Will you be okay?"

"I'll be fine." In my years, I had traveled in less comfortable and expensive ways. Her purse smelled of new leather. It was filled with many other different fragrances, a scented handkerchief, a bottle of Chanel No. 5, and the subtle scent of nettle leaves. Her heels clicked on the marble entry floor of the police station. There were muffled conversations. "Mr. Bridgestone, thank you for coming so quickly."

"Of course, Emma," came the soft-spoken, slow speech of a southern gentleman.

"This is my friend, Beatrice Twiggs. Beatrice, this is my longtime family attorney, William Bridgestone."

"Nice to meet you. I spoke with the desk sergeant. Abigail is being detained for questioning in detention. She has not been charged yet."

Mrs. Twiggs interrupted. "We have to get her out of here."

As I listened to the conversation, a shadow passed over me. I'm not much for premonitions. That is not one of my powers, but I knew Abigail would not last the night in this place. She was vulnerable without her companions around to protect her. "May we see her?" Mrs. Twiggs asked.

"Yes, I've made arrangements."

I followed the footsteps in my mind's eyes, down the hallway, turning right and then left, stopping and hearing the clicking of the door, a female voice, a young officer who, I imagined, was speaking with the attorney. And then the door closed behind us. I could smell Abigail. I could smell her fear.

Mrs. Tangledwood put her purse on the floor. I leapt out and wrapped myself around Abigail's leg. She scratched my head. "Be strong, Abigail," I told her. Mrs. Tangledwood introduced Abigail to her attorney.

Mr. Bridgestone spoke. "The police have you in the vicinity the night of Lionel Foret's murder behind the Leaf & Page. And they found your phone number in Bryson Wald's phone."

"What are you talking about?" Abigail asked.

Mrs. Twiggs placed her hand over her mouth. "Oh my dear, they didn't tell you?"

"Tell me what? No one's told me anything." Abigail crossed her arms over her chest.

"Bryson Wald was found dead last night in the alley behind the Orange Peel," Mr. Bridgestone said. "He was killed with the same weapon that was used to kill Lionel Foret."

Abigail stopped breathing. "Be strong," I told her again.

"Where were you last night?" the attorney asked.

"I was at the Orange Peel waiting for Bryson. He never showed up."

"Have you told that to the police?"

"I haven't said anything to them."

Mr. Bridgestone cleared his throat.

Mrs. Twiggs said, "If she hasn't been charged, they can't keep her, can they? Can she go home?"

"They can hold her for twenty-four hours and then decide if she will be charged or not," Mr. Bridgestone said. "There's nothing I can do until they decide whether or not to charge her. We'll talk more tomorrow."

"Abigail, listen to me very carefully. I'm going to stay with you tonight." I spoke into her mind.

"Terra, how?"

"I want you to trust me and clear your mind tonight like we did together and meet me in the clarity. There I am as I was, and whatever powers I had as a witch are strong."

"Terra, I can't get there without you."

"You can, Abigail. You're capable of so much more than you know. Trust me. I will reach out to you."

I stopped talking. I was afraid Abigail would hear the voices that were speaking to me, the dark voices that filled the small holding room, darting out from the corners, slithering from the shadows, hissing, "We're coming for you, Abigail."

I climbed back into Mrs. Tangledwood's purse. The last words I left hanging in the air were, "Be strong, Abigail."

A FREE SPIRIT

I CHECKED THE CLOCK OVER THE cash register. It was nearly nine p.m. Mrs. Twiggs was told that was when the lights were extinguished in the holding cells at the police station. I had tried for nearly an hour to reach out to Abigail without success. I felt her safe as long as the fluorescent lights hummed overhead. Not that those dark creatures couldn't reach out in the light but more because Abigail felt safer with the lights on. The unseen is always scarier than the seen, and foul creatures prey more easily on the weak.

Mrs. Twiggs paced up and down in front of the cash register, mumbling to herself. Mrs. Tangledwood sat by the fire, reading a book, Pixel in her lap.

"Terra, I've been reading something very interesting about transfixation. Actually that's not what it's called here, but I believe it's the same principle," Mrs. Tangledwood said.

I leapt onto the back of Mrs. Tanglewood's chair to see what she was reading. I was surprised to see it was written in Mandarin.

"Oh, yes, Terra, I can speak and read several languages. This is an original copy of the philosopher Tse-uhe's writing Mrs. Twiggs found for me. He came to America during the railroad boom. He wrote journals about the Chinese laborers who came over to build the Trans-Pacific line. He was somewhat of a shaman to them. He practiced wu, the spirit medium of the ancient Chinese sorcerers. There's an interesting passage here about a Chinese laborer who was caught in an avalanche of falling rocks while placing dynamite in a tunnel. He was buried alive for many days. Tse-uhe describes how he was able to communicate with the buried worker telepathically to help keep him alive. He used spirit bowls filled with different liquids. By rubbing his finger along the rim, he tuned in to find the right frequency to connect with the laborer's spirit."

"Mrs. Tangledwood, I've tried reaching Abigail. I was able to lock in her frequency when she was sitting across from me, but I cannot reach out to her now. Something is blocking me," I said.

"Tse-uhe had the same problem with the trapped man. The frequency could not penetrate through granite."

A flash of understanding came across me. It was not the distance that was blocking my call to Abigail or the solid limestone walls of the jail. It was the voices I heard in the police station. They were screaming at Abigail, blocking her from hearing me. She couldn't hear them when she was awake and the lights were on, but they were there in her subconscious in the shadows. When the lights turn off, the boogieman under the bed becomes real. Her imagination would wander, drawing the voices in, and then they would devour her.

I turned to Mrs. Tangledwood. "How did Tse-uhe reach the laborer?"

"He left his body and entered the trapped man's body."

I jumped off the back of the chair. Elizabeth had warned me to never attempt that level of transfixation. Leaving your consciousness was one level of transfixation—your spirit stayed in your body protected—but transfixing your true light, what the humans call your spirit, and leaving your body, left you unprotected. Like Elizabeth, if my earthly body was destroyed, I would be floating in the atmosphere, lost for eternity. Pixel jumped on my back. "What's wrong, Terra? Terra, you scared. Pixel here. Pixel help Terra." Uncontrollably I started licking the back of Pixel's head, cleaning his fur. I didn't even stop to think how disgusting that was. It seemed catlike.

"Pixel, I'm leaving for a little while."

"Pixel come too." He sat, not leaving me an argument.

"No, Pixel, you can't follow me."

"Pixel go where Terra go. No more talk."

"Pixel, I'm going to sleep for a while." I stopped trying to figure out how to explain transfixation to Pixel. I began again. "I'm going to dream and visit Abigail and stay with her tonight, but I need you to watch over me."

"Pixel no understand. You sleep, you here."

"Pixel, you have to promise me you will not leave my side while I sleep no matter what happens. Okay? Can you do that for Terra?"

"I will not leave Terra." Pixel lay on top of me. I closed my eyes. When we were young girls, seven or eight years old, Prudence and I borrowed Elizabeth's book of spells, our girlish curiosity having gotten the better of us. We stole away into the woods on a summer afternoon, pretending we were one of the old ones, the great witches who once walked the earth. We sat for hours, staring at the book too afraid to open it. It was Prudence who finally found the courage. As she unsnapped the clasp, the book flipped like a zoetrope, giving the illustrations the illusion of motion. The pages stopped on a chapter titled Transfixation. We huddled together, holding hands and reading the incantation out loud. Before we could finish, we felt our bodies being lifted off the ground—being pulled by our hair—by Elizabeth.

"Prudence, Terra, you wicked girls." She scooped up the book and never said another word about it.

As Pixel kept watch, I recited that incantation, and then I left my body behind.

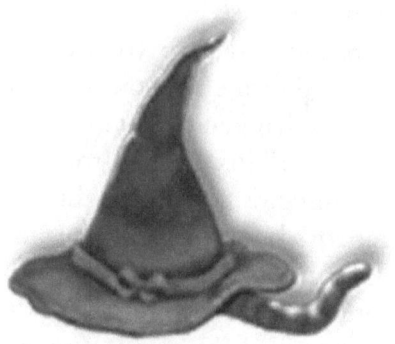

WINDOWS TO THE SOUL

I STOOD IN THE SHADOWS, THE mist floating around me, engulfing me. Memories swirled around me, some were my own, some belonged to others. A familiar voice whispered, "Terra." Elizabeth appeared in the mist. She hugged me and then pulled back. "You wicked girl. What have you done?" she scolded me.

"Elizabeth, I've searched for you for more than three hundred years."

"I've always been with you, Terra."

"Is this real, Elizabeth? Are you real?"

"The world you left behind with your body is the dream. This is reality. This is as it was and as it will be."

"Elizabeth, I have so many questions for you. Please tell me how can I turn back into my former self?"

Elizabeth flickered and pixelated. "Terra, it's coming." And then she was gone.

I found myself in Abigail's cell. The fluorescent lights dimmed before extinguishing. The hissing shadows turned into screams. Abigail sat curled up on the corner of her cot, huddled under a blanket, rocking back and forth, her hands covering her ears. Elizabeth had once told me the eyes are the windows to the soul, I believed that phrase meant we are what we see, but there is more to it. The ancient Egyptians placed gold coins on the eyelids of the dead to pay the ferryman who would lead them across the river Styx but also to keep lost souls from entering and reanimating the body. "I am with you," I screamed above the voices to Abigail.

She opened her eyes. She saw my true light and took it into her body. "Terra, I can feel you inside me."

"I'm here to protect you, Abigail. Don't be afraid. Be strong."

"The screams, Terra, they're maddening. Make them stop. Make them stop."

I could feel tentacles and talons scraping at our body. Flesh tearing. I raised Abigail's hands. Through her, I was a witch again. I screamed. "Darkness fear the light. I am Terra Rowan."

A bright light exploded from Abigail's fingertips. Distorted creatures screamed in agony and slithered into the crevices hidden within the walls. "Rest now, Abigail. I will keep watch. You are safe." I could feel our body was exhausted. She lay down. I sang to her until she fell asleep. I kept one eye open.

"Terra, breathe, Terra."

I sat upright, gasping air. My heart began beating again.

"Terra, dead. Terra, dead." Pixel's voice filled my ears and then he licked me frantically on my head.

I blinked my eyes. "Where am I, Pixel?"

"Terra, bad things. Hurt Terra."

I glanced around. It took me a minute to recognize my surroundings. We were in the alley behind the Leaf & Page, hidden behind the dumpster. I shook my head. "How'd we get here?"

"Terra, me pull Terra. Me save you."

"Save me from what?"

"Inside dark." Pixel stuttered.

"You okay, Pixel?"

"It comes. Take you."

I tried looking inside Pixel's mind, but I could not pierce the veil. Instead, I hugged him. "Thank you, Pixel."

"Me hungry." He jumped off the garbage cans onto the kitchen windowsill and scratched the pane. Mrs. Twiggs opened the window.

"What are you two doing out there? Come on in and eat before we open." She let us in the back door.

Pixel wandered through her legs, meowing softly. I heard him chanting, "Bacon. Bacon. Bacon." Seemingly to understand him, Mrs. Twiggs placed a plate of steaming bacon on the floor. I, too, was ravenous. My body had taken quite a shock. As we ate, I watched Mrs. Twiggs wind the cuckoo clock above the cash register and whisper good morning to her picture of Albert.

"My, look at the time," she said, then flipped the sign from closed to open. Mrs. Tangledwood came down the stairs.

"I just spoke to Mr. Bridgestone. They're going to release Abigail today. They don't have enough evidence to charge her," she said.

ABIGAIL'S RELEASE

PIXEL AND I WAITED OUTSIDE the police station. My head pounded. All my joints were on fire. It was the first time in my life as either a witch or a cat that I felt the effects of age. Leaving my body had spent my life source. I would never be the same.

It was lunchtime, and the square was bustling with traffic. Cars circled, searching for elusive parking spaces, people streamed by on their way to one of the many downtown eateries. Pixel and I stood by the statue of George Vanderbilt across from the police station. My head felt fuzzy. I felt as though I was drifting between two worlds. Something that Elizabeth said still bothered me, that this world was the dream and the other reality. I couldn't imagine what she meant.

Mrs. Tangledwood flung open the door followed by Mrs. Twiggs and a disheveled Abigail. She was pale white. She, too, was spent from the night. She walked past me and climbed into Mrs. Tangledwood's Bentley without acknowledging me. I was confused. Why was she ignoring me? Mrs. Twiggs opened the back door to let Pixel and me in. Then she climbed in beside us. We all rode in silence until Mrs. Twiggs found her voice.

"I've fixed a room for you over the store until you feel better."

"I want to get out of this city," Abigail said, her arms wrapped around herself.

Abigail gave Mrs. Tangledwood directions to the cabin, as no GPS of this world could lead us there. The dirt road up the side of

Black Mountain is a treacherous route by car. At times the narrow path was only as wide as the width of the Bentley's axles. A sheer drop a hundred feet into the gulley kept unwanted visitors away, and magic kept away the rest. We reached the stream, and the Bentley came to a dead stop.

"What's wrong?" Mrs. Twiggs asked from the back seat.

"The stream is swollen. The road is washed out," Abigail said.

I jumped up onto the headrest to see for myself. It was as Abigail said, no way to pass. It had not rained in days, and we had easily traversed the shallow stream that circled the cabin just a few nights ago.

"I can walk from here," Abigail said as she opened the door and walked toward the water.

Mrs. Tangledwood looked over her shoulder at me. I then whispered in her ear, "Tomorrow night," which she understood. "She'll be fine. Thank you for the ride," I said.

Pixel and I caught up to Abigail, who was sitting on a log near the water's edge. I could hear the Bentley's tires kicking up stones as it headed back down the mountain. Abigail stood up and walked into the water or onto the water. Her boots glided along the top of the fast-moving stream, never dipping beneath the surface. I looked down to the bottom; it was nearly four or maybe five feet deep. Pixel dove in. His belly bounced off the tips of the white caps, and then he was upright and walking on water next to Abigail. I followed. We reached the cabin at twilight, exhausted. Abigail fell onto the cot and covered herself.

Pixel looked at me with sad eyes. "Terra, me worried."

"Sleep, Pixel. I'll keep watch."

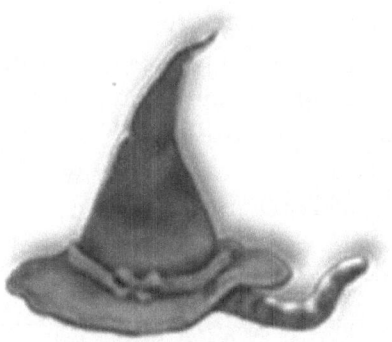

TRACKER

"ME SCARED. TERRA GONE. ME scared." Pixel's cries reached my ears as I crossed the stream back to our cabin. The minute he saw me, he ran, knocking me over and biting my neck. He knocked the squirming trout out of my mouth. "You home. You home."

"Pixel, I just went to find food," I told him.

"Abigail no feel good."

"Yes, I know. Pixel, I'm going to need your help," I said, pushing him off me.

"Me help?"

"Yes, we're having a gathering tonight."

"Party?" Pixel asked.

"Sort of."

"Cookies?"

"Yes, like at Mrs. Twiggs, a gathering of the Biltmore ladies."

"Smell funny," Pixel said.

"Yes, the ladies with the perfume."

"Pixel no like."

"Pixel, this is very important. We need the ladies to help us with Abigail. I'm counting on you."

"Me familiar."

"Yes, Pixel, you're my familiar and I trust you."

"Pixel love Terra."

"Thank you, Pixel," I told him as we approached the cabin.

Abigail came outside, stretching and yawning. "Where have you been? Pixel has been yelling and grunting all morning."

"You need to eat. You need to regain your strength," I told her. "Mrs. Tangledwood is calling a special meeting of the Biltmore Society. They're coming to the cabin tonight."

"Why the cabin?" Abigail asked.

"There's no time for me to discern which of the ladies, if any, are Wiccans and whether they have white or black magic. If they carry black magic, I will need to be prepared to control them."

"How do you plan on doing that?"

"Agatha Hollows taught me how to control black Wiccans. Unlike the peaceful human Wiccans, the bloodline of black Wiccans flows from dark magic. The mountain folk thought they were possessed or crazy, but Agatha knew the truth and knew how to take their power." I thought for a moment. "We better prepare. First we gather the necessary herbs and plants. Once the Wiccans' powers awake—if they are dark powers—they will want to hide from us. We must see through their disguise."

"I thought you told me that I was the first human you've spoken to since turning into a cat."

"I never said Agatha Hollows was human."

Abigail became silent.

"Do you want to talk about what happened last night?"

"No, I don't." Abigail donned her boots and stepped off the porch. I led her around back to the remains of Agatha Hollows's herb and flower garden. While all her plantings were overgrown, they were still useful.

"That one." I held a paw up to a tall purple foxglove.

"Foxglove are poisonous," Abigail said.

"Not if used properly. You need a very small amount to help wake the Wiccan blood," I told Abigail.

Using gardening shears, she snipped off a few flowers and placed them in the basket she had draped over her arm. We continued walking through the garden.

I pulled out some Saint-John's-wort. "What's this for?" Abigail asked.

"Saint-John's-wort contains hypericin. It's a photosensitory substance that reacts with light. In some people, it causes skin burns, but in black Wiccans, it hyper-reacts causing extreme burns. Darkness hides from the light."

"Okay." Abigail shrugged.

Pixel scampered about, chasing butterflies throughout the garden. "Me happy. Me happy," he chanted.

I pointed to a patch of light blue flowers. "Those are called Indian tobacco. When ground into a powder, humans use this plant to help with respiratory problems. Agatha Hollows used it to help the mountain folk with bronchitis and bad colds. In our potion, it expands the lungs raising the oxygen levels in the blood. It releases their Wiccan DNA."

A scream rang out through the field. I turned to see Pixel sitting upright, the tracker standing over him, his teeth bared. I was wrong about him, and my mistake could cost Pixel his life. I ran as fast as I could, but before I could pounce on the tracker, the rattlesnake he was protecting Pixel from lunged and bit the puppy. He yelped and ran toward the stream. I grabbed the snake by the back of its head, but before I could kill it, Abigail pulled a knife from her boot and cut its head off. Pixel cried, "Tracker, good, Tracker, good. Help Tracker."

Abigail and I followed the path Tracker had laid down in the tall brush. We followed him for miles until finally we found him lying down, covered in mud on the bank of the French Broad River. He had known that the mud would help extract some of the venom. Abigail bent over the small puppy. His breath was shallow, his tongue hanging out. "I have to get him to the vet," she said, gathering him in her arms.

"There's no time for that. Reach in your basket and take out the mayapple. Crush it and put it on his wound. Witches use mayapple for poison. They call it witches' umbrella. Agatha Hollows told me the Cherokee used it to treat snakebites."

Abigail followed my instructions. The puppy lifted his head and licked her hand. He stood up, his long legs ungainly under his oversized paws. This pup couldn't be more than a few months old. "This stuff is remarkable."

"It's not the mayapple. It doesn't work that quickly, and honestly I was only trying to slow the venom so we could get him to the doctor. It's you. You did this." I stared at her with a newfound respect and fear. She was more powerful than I had thought. Even Elizabeth would have needed a stronger potion to save this dog.

Abigail washed the puppy with the river water, scooped him up, and carried him back to the cabin. Pixel was waiting on the porch.

"Tracker, Tracker," he exclaimed, circling around Abigail.

While the puppy could not be more than six months old, he was at least a good forty pounds. Recognizing his mottled fur, I realized I'd seen this breed before. Agatha Hollows raised what she called Australian shepherds, she said because they were the smartest of the dog creatures. She trained them to pick herbs and medicine sticks and to protect the cabin. After she died, the remaining dogs took off into the wild. I knew this puppy was from their bloodline because of his russet red coat and his brilliant blue eyes. Ghost eyes, Agatha Hollows had called them. They kept their distance from me and I from them, but I did admire their intelligence. Unlike some of the dogs I'd met over the past three hundred years, these dogs had no problem understanding and accepting me, although it did bother me the way they stared deep into my soul. This puppy was the last of his bloodline. For that he deserved to live.

Abigail was in the rocking chair, cradling the puppy and singing softly. Pixel grabbed a piece of beef jerky out of Abigail's backpack and presented it to the tracker. "Me friend, Tracker me friend." The tracker licked Pixel's head before nibbling at his ear. Pixel giggled and fell on his back laughing.

"Terra, you know this dog, don't you?" Abigail asked.

"I've never seen him, but I've felt his presence."

"When was that?"

"The first night I brought you here. I thought he was tracking me, but he must have been tracking you."

Abigail studied the dog that was now sound asleep on her lap. "Tracker, that's what I will call you. Tracker," she said.

"Tracker, Tracker, Tracker," Pixel sang triumphantly, dancing around in circles before doing a somersault on the floor.

"We have to finish before the ladies get here," I said.

A car pulled up onto the long dirt path. Mrs. Tangledwood leapt out and ran around to the passenger side to help Mrs. Twiggs. Mrs. Tangledwood looked even younger than when I had seen her the day before. Her power was growing. She would be our greatest weapon against the gathering storm. I greeted them on the porch.

"Terra, I've brought the herbs and teas for the turning just like we made at the Leaf & Page," Mrs. Twiggs said. "And this." She pulled out a silver carving knife.

Abigail stepped up behind us. "What's that for?"

"Just in case," I told her.

I felt bad for Mrs. Twiggs. I wished the potion had worked for her. Out of all the people I've met during my long life, I trusted her most. There was a kindness in her, a selflessness that would not allow her to be anything but a good person. But for now I needed magic. We worked quickly into the early evening.

"Abigail, how did you come across this cabin?" Mrs. Tangled-wood asked.

"Terra brought me here."

"It's interesting. I am on the board of the Asheville Historical Museum. I've never seen any mention of this cabin."

"Terra told me the woman who lived here was a mountain medicine woman during the Civil War."

"I'd love to get more information on the woman who lived here for the museum."

Agatha Hollows never told me where she came from or who she was. She could understand me but never wanted to talk. I knew her true self. She was a Cherokee medicine woman, a descendant of the old ones. She wore a tear dress like the ones worn by the Cherokee women driven out of North Carolina on the trail of tears. She came to Black Mountain to escape the soldiers when the Civil War broke out. She enchanted the cabin so it could only be found if it wished to be found. I spoke to the cabin in Chero-kee, asking her to let the ladies find her. A deep sigh released from her walls. Agatha was wont to keep visitors away.

Abigail lit a fire as the sun melted behind the mountain ridge. Tracker stayed glued to her side following her every movement, walking between her legs as she walked. His light blue eyes constantly gazing up at her. I could tell Pixel was a bit jealous. He tried to climb up her leg. Tracker pushed him out of the way.

"Abigail, whose dog is this?" Mrs. Tangledwood asked, stepping away from Tracker.

"He's a stray I've been feeding," Abigail said, petting Tracker's head.

Mrs. Tangledwood reached down to rub Tracker's ears, but he backed away. "Terra," Mrs. Tangledwood said. "When I turned, I felt a great energy being released within me. I felt limitless. Will the ladies feel the same way? Will they be as powerful as me?"

"Each Wiccan will have their own special powers, but it's up to you to develop them, to make them stronger," Terra said.

"How do I do that?"

"By learning spells, sharpening your skills, understanding your abilities."

"I don't know what my abilities are."

I could see Mrs. Tangledwood's aura glowing around her in bright shades of green. She had the power of rejuvenation, not just for herself but for anything she willed. I was still uncertain if I should share this knowledge with her. It might be better that she discovered it herself. Mrs. Tangledwood picked up some twigs for the fire, and as she did, tiny buds sprouted on the branches, turning into leaves. She stood and stared in awe and then dropped the branches.

We all stood staring at them as cars pulled up the path. Pixel ran to the porch, exclaiming, "They here."

Tracker let out a low puppy growl and lay down on Abigail's feet, protecting her already.

I turned to my companions and said, "Whatever happens here tonight has to stay here in this cabin." Abigail understood what I meant. Behind her back, I could see the glint of the silver knife. We couldn't unleash a black Wiccan into the world and into my Asheville.

Tracker growled and leapt up to the front window. Abigail stood next to him, petting his head, whispering in his ear. He lay down. Agatha Hollows had placed enchantments on the gnarled bristle-cone pines that lined the path from the stream to the cabin. Their strong arms outstretched crisscrossing barring entrance. Tracker had heard what Pixel and I heard. The cracking of the limbs as they gave way to the ladies of the Biltmore Society.

Mrs. Twiggs stood on the porch, greeting each lady as they came up the steps, each asking about the purpose of the meeting. Mrs. Twiggs had been very careful not to give it away.

Mrs. Tangledwood stood in the kitchen, finishing the potion, her back to the room. When she turned around, they stopped dead, gasping at the sight of her. They turned to each other, mumbling in disbelief. "It's me, Emma," Mrs. Tangledwood said.

"Emma, that can't be you. You're beautiful," Mrs. Stickman stuttered. "What's going on here?" She turned to Mrs. Twiggs.

"The reason we invited you here: Emma is a Wiccan, and her powers have been awakened. We have reason to believe that the ladies of the Biltmore Society were brought together by powers we don't yet understand. Tonight we're going to attempt to awaken those powers," Mrs. Twiggs said.

"What about you, Beatrice? You haven't changed at all."

"That's because I'm not a Wiccan. I believe it's because I wasn't born in Biltmore Forest. You and your lineage go back hundreds of years to this land. That bloodline is where your powers lie."

"What do we have to do?" Mrs. Stickman asked.

"Find a chair in the circle." As the ladies took their places, Tracker walked by each one, sniffing, peering into their souls with his ghost blue eyes. He finally settled down in the corner by the wood stove. I stepped into the middle of the circle.

"So, it is true, the cat can communicate," Mrs. Stickman said.

"I can understand her now. She's a witch. She wants you to drink the same potion that I drank," Mrs. Tangledwood told them, standing next to me.

Abigail came in from the kitchen, carrying a tea service. She placed it on the small table in the center of the circle. She poured seven cups. Mrs. Stickman stared. "That's it. We drink the tea and we all become Wiccans?" she asked. "Is it dangerous?"

I turned and faced them, shaking my head no. She smiled back.

I have to say that I relayed a bit of a half truth because it was not the same potion that Mrs. Twiggs and Mrs. Tangledwood drank. This one was poison to a black Wiccan. No matter the outcome, Abigail would make sure that if there were a black Wiccan, she wouldn't leave this cabin.

"Any magic words?" Mrs. Stickman asked.

I shook my head again. Abigail sat down in the rocker by the hearth, Tracker at her feet. She picked up her guitar and strummed it softly to calm her nerves. Though by some lost instinct or memory she played the song—my coven's song. The room began to spin. The faces around me melted like paraffin wax into puddles as the voices returned in my head. I thought at first they had drunk the tea and all were found to be black Wiccans, but then I heard Elizabeth's voice.

"Terra, put the lantern out," she told me, stepping back from the barn door as I opened it.

"But Elizabeth."

"Terra, now and close the door."

I did as she commanded. The full moon filtered in through the slats of the barn. Elizabeth stood in the shadows.

"What's wrong, Elizabeth?" I asked. "You're scaring me."

She walked into the slivers of moonlight. Her condition gave her away, the swelling of her belly answered my question. "Terra, I'm with child. With Jonathan Goodall's child."

"Oh, Elizabeth, no."

She took my hand and placed it on her belly. I could feel her daughter kick. Elizabeth smiled. "Yes, it is a girl. I love Jonathan, Terra."

"Does he know?"

"I can no longer keep it hidden. The time has come, and we must leave town. We plan to leave tonight."

"Elizabeth, how will you survive? Where will you go?"

"Jonathan has confidants in the French colony of La Louisiane."

"That's the wilderness. It's so far away."

"It has to be this way. I need you, my dear Terra." Elizabeth took both my hands in hers. "To lead the coven."

"Me? I'm not ready. I haven't wanded yet."

"Terra, you're the only one I trust. You have to do this." She doubled over in pain, clutching her stomach.

"Elizabeth, what's wrong?"

"The hour grows near." She clenched my hand, her fingers cutting off the circulation in mine. Elizabeth's familiar howled in the distance. She ran to the window, peeking out. She reached in the pocket of her cape and placed something in the palm of my hand and closed it around. "Terra, take this."

"What is it? What is it, Elizabeth?"

"It's a chance for new life if anything happens to me." The howl grew louder, and with it human voices sounded in the distance. Elizabeth looked out the window again; I stood behind her and saw the flickering of lanterns coming out of the woods toward the farm. She grasped her belly, wincing in pain.

"Elizabeth," I called out again.

She reached in the hope chest, rifling through its contents. She turned, her face pale white. "Terra, it's gone."

"What's gone, Elizabeth?"

"The book." Her eyes rolled back into her head. She began to faint. I caught her and laid her onto the hay. She screamed in pain. "Terra, something's wrong. The baby's coming."

"Elizabeth, I'll fetch the midwife." I darted toward the door.

Elizabeth pulled me back. "No, no one must know. You can do this, Terra."

I grabbed a horse blanket and covered Elizabeth. She stifled her screams. With my eyes almost closed, my heart pounding, I looked under her dress. Through the faint glow of the lantern, I could see the baby's head. Moments later I held her daughter as I cut her birth cord. I wrapped the baby in a cloth torn from my petticoat and placed her on Elizabeth's chest.

"She's beautiful, Elizabeth," I said as the baby cried softly.

Elizabeth smiled. In the distance, her familiar howled again. This time the voices sounded nearer. "We don't have much time. Our secret's been told, Terra. Black magic is gathering in the woods. Our hour is late. If you don't control it, it will control you. Find the book before it finds you. Save the coven," Elizabeth said. I ran to the window. I could see the lanterns were coming closer. The barn door burst open. I grabbed for a pitchfork. The silhouette of a man stood in the doorway. Jonathan Goodall ran to Elizabeth's side and embraced her. He stared down at his daughter. "Take her, Jonathan, before they do," Elizabeth said.

"Elizabeth, come with us," he said, smoothing Elizabeth's sweat-stained hair.

"I'm too weak. They're too close. Just take her. I'll come to you," Elizabeth gasped out. She reached around her neck, releasing the clasp on her amulet. She placed it in his hand and drew him close, whispering in his ear. She kissed him passionately.

Jonathan wrapped the baby in his cloak, brushed her cheek, and kissed her.

"Guard our daughter, Jonathan, keep her safe," Elizabeth gasped out.

Jonathan ran to the door, gave one last glance at Elizabeth, and disappeared into the darkness, protecting his precious bundle.

I stared out the window. I could now see the faces of the angry townspeople. "Elizabeth, we have to go. We have to hide."

"You can hide from the humans but not from it. Run, Terra,

run," she told me.

"Not without you, Elizabeth. Come with me."

"There's no time. You must run to save our coven."

With one last glance at Elizabeth, I stepped out of the barn, careful to search all around me, making sure no one saw me. I hoped to move among the shadows, but the full moon gave me away. I ran into the woods, tripping over a fallen branch. Around me the bushes shook. I screamed, then covered my mouth and ran toward the ocean.

"Terra, Terra." I heard Abigail's voice, and then I heard Mrs. Stickman and Mrs. Bowers. They were all there in my head, standing over me. I opened my eyes and saw the seven had turned to white Wiccans. I closed my eyes again, my head pounding. I reopened my eyes to see the faces of the once elderly ladies of the Biltmore Society. Gray hair turned obsidian black, wrinkled skin now smooth and rosy cheeked. The years had been erased away. The telltale sign of a true Wiccan, their irises flashed traces of fire red in their excitement. Their chattering voices echoed in my head.

"Settle down, ladies. This is the beginning," Mrs. Tangledwood said. "We've got a lot to learn and a short time to learn it. Terra tells me there is black magic descending on Asheville, and she needs our help to find and destroy it."

Mrs. Stickman half listened as she admired her hands. What were once gnarled and arthritic were supple and strong. She lifted the teakettle and glanced at her reflection in the polished copper. "I'm beautiful," she said with a smile. "I haven't looked this good since my forties. In fact, I don't think I looked this good in my forties. I feel so alive."

"What you're seeing is your true self and because you believe this is how you should look others see you that way. Understand it is somewhat of an illusion. You are still the same woman you were before," I told her.

"Does that mean we're going to change back? We're going to age again?" Mrs. Stickman asked, setting down the teakettle.

"As long as you accept your true self and believe you look this way, you will stay as you are now."

"What about our powers? I feel like I can do anything," Mrs. Bowers said.

"I can help you develop your individual strengths. For now you must rest. The turning spends your health. Go home, get a good night's sleep, and we'll begin your training in the morrow."

Mrs. Twiggs handed each lady a stone on a leather string. "This is blue chalcedony. It's found throughout the mountains here. It will protect you against black magic."

"Where did you get these?" Mrs. Stickman asked.

"The woman who owned this cabin had them buried in the backyard. Terra told us where to find them."

The ladies each examined their new talisman as Mrs. Twiggs walked them out of the cabin. I heard Mrs. Stickman whisper, "When do we get our brooms?" I realized they have a lot to learn.

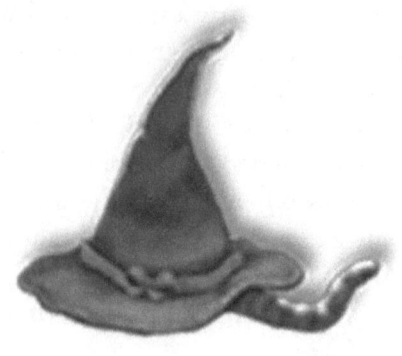

LIFTING THE VEIL

I WOKE BEFORE THE OTHERS. TRACKER was cuddled up with Abigail on the cot. Pixel lay next to the smoldering fire, kicking his paws in a dream. "Shiny, shiny knife. No, no hurt, no hurt Pixel."

"Pixel, are you okay?" I nudged him awake, licking his ear.

Pixel's orange saucer eyes popped wide open. "Bad. Bad, Terra."

"Pixel, what did you remember?"

I could see the fading remnants of his dream still lingering in his eyes. It was the alley where Lionel was killed and the shadow of a figure turning into the walkway. I saw the moon's reflection in the silver knife the killer held. "It's okay, Pixel, it's just a dream."

"Bad dream," Pixel said, nuzzling up against me. And then the vision was gone. Pixel was back. "Me hungry, me hungry."

"Let's go catch breakfast, Pixel."

Tracker's head lifted from the bed as we exited the cabin. He started to follow us, then turned to glance at Abigail. I looked over my shoulder, gave him a glance which he understood to mean protect her, keep watch. He let out a low growl and then lay back down. "Terra, fish," Pixel said as we stepped off the porch.

"Yes, Pixel, we'll catch some fish for breakfast. First I want to show you something." I headed to the far end of Agatha Hollows's land where she used to dig up ginseng. She had told me of its ability to restore memory especially when black magic was fogging the mind as she called it. "Pixel, I want you to smell along the ground here."

"Me smell. What me smell for?"

"It's called ginseng. It's a root."

"It smell like?"

"It will have a dirty, earthy smell and a spicy smell."

"Me no like spice."

I dug up a small piece of ginseng. "Smell this, Pixel."

"Mm, me eat?" Pixel said.

"Pixel, this will help you remember what happened in the alley."

"No, bad." Pixel stepped back.

"Pixel, it's safe." I knew from my years with Agatha that the herbs and roots in these mountains have a frequency that matches any ailment. Agatha Hollows taught me many remedies using these herbs. In Pixel's case, it's the shadow over his memory. I knew that Pixel would not understand, so I commanded him, "Pixel, eat."

Pixel jumped back, away from the root. "No, no, Pixel, no like. Pixel no like ginseng."

"Pixel you have to trust me. You're my familiar. You have to do what I say."

"Pixel familiar."

"Yes."

"Me trust Terra."

"Nibble a little on the root. Not too much." I pushed it toward him with my paw.

Pixel reluctantly took a bite and swallowed hard. "No, good. No taste good."

I knew something was keeping Pixel from remembering what happened the night Lionel was murdered. I couldn't identify what black magic was blocking his memory, and for that reason I couldn't reverse it. "Pixel, I need you to help me now, okay?"

"Terra, yes."

"Think about your favorite things. Concentrate very, very hard. Okay, can you do that for Terra?"

Pixel formed images in his head, most were of food, but there was one of me, then of Mrs. Twiggs followed by Abigail followed by Tracker. As he concentrated on those images like a vacuum sucking the air out of his head, I could see the dark shadows follow, engulfing those images, strangling the light out of them. As they did, I could see behind them into what they were hiding. I could see the silver blade plunging into Lionel's chest. His eyes bulging from the pain. I could see Lionel's deep midnight-blue aura light fading like a vapor trail. I could not see his killer. It hurt my head to even try. Its shape had no form, just a constantly moving mass of darkness. It was like looking through a Vaseline-covered lens. The apparition turned and looked right at me. It knew I was looking at it. I could see the outline of a black hood and a storm cloud forming where a face should be. Particles flew around in a cyclone trying to pull together the face but remained fragmentary.

"Run, Terra, run," Elizabeth's voice echoed in my head. I stood still for a moment, watching her, hesitant. "Run, Terra," she repeated more urgently. I raced across the field. I felt someone watching me from behind the trees. I couldn't make anything out through the dark. The darkness hid the shadow that followed me. I stopped for a moment, stranded between vision and memory. It was there the night Elizabeth gave birth. All I could make out was the black cape and the sheen of silver. I realized that the black magic was watching my memories; it was part of my memory.

I shuddered as Pixel moaned. It brought me back to his vision. The dark figure held a blade pointing up at me. My blood went cold. My breath left me. My heart stopped. The black magic was reaching out to me, pulling me back into the shadows. I couldn't look any longer.

"Terra, eat now. Me hungry."

"What? What'd you say, Pixel?" I shook my head, falling to the ground.

Pixel jumped on top of me, biting my neck. "No play now, we eat. Pixel hungry."

"Yes, Pixel. Let's go get breakfast." I shook off my vision and followed Pixel as he scampered along to the stream.

On the way he singsonged, "Hungry, hungry, Pixel, hungry," on his way.

When we had finished, we headed back to the cabin, Pixel carrying a large trout for Abigail. She sat on the porch, cradling a cup of tea. Tracker ran around the front yard, chasing bees. "What do we do now, Terra?" she asked.

"First we eat, and then we talk about the Wiccans," I told her as Pixel dropped the fish at her feet.

"Why didn't you have me drink the tea? You keep saying I'm special. That there's some reason you and I are together. Maybe I'm a Wiccan too."

"You're not a Wiccan, Abigail." I followed Pixel into the cabin before she could ask any more questions.

After we ate, Abigail counted her change. "I need to get my mother's watch back," she said, putting the money into her pocket.

"We'll head into town to get your watch. First I want to stop at Mrs. Twiggs's," I said. The four of us took the well-worn path back to Biltmore Village. Pixel chased bumblebees along the way. Tracker obliging to help with the hunt, shook his head furiously when he got stung.

We arrived at the Leaf & Page as Mrs. Twiggs was clearing the breakfast dishes from the café tables. Mrs. Tangledwood sat by the fire, reading a book. She looked even younger than when we had seen her the night before. I jumped onto the arm of the wing-back chair to see what she was reading. I cricked my head around to the front of the book. In faded gold letter, it read, *Spellbound*. It was a very old book. I could smell the years of water damage, the acid from the yellow paper, but what really caught my nose was the smell of old blood. The book had been used in a ceremony.

"Oh, hello, Terra dear." Mrs. Tangledwood pulled her nose out of the book. "Just doing some light reading. You know, I've been collecting books on magic and the occult for years. I thought them interesting fantasy, but these are instruction manuals." She closed the book. "I'm fascinated by the legends of the Biltmore Society and Olmsted's studies on the paranormal. Now I know that magic is real."

"I thought that was the purpose of the ladies of the Biltmore Society to preserve the magic of the forest," I said.

Mrs. Tangledwood put the book down and let out a hearty laugh. "Oh, no, Terra, the purpose of the ladies of the Biltmore Society is to drink tea and the occasional moonshine. Gossip about our neighbors and keep ourselves as the exclusive society of the daughters of the founding families."

"Mrs. Twiggs takes it very seriously," I said.

"Beatrice is a wonderful woman, but she's not really one of us. She wasn't born here."

"I'd be careful with that book until you understand your powers," I told her.

Mrs. Tangledwood smiled and lifted her right hand, pinky in the air as though she was holding a very delicate teacup. From the kitchen, one of Mrs. Twiggs's precious Rosenthal teacups flew to her on command. I watched as the cup filled itself with a breakfast tea, but the smell was sickly sweet. Too much sugar, I thought. Mrs. Tangledwood took a sip, not noticing the odor.

I climbed up the back of her chair and put my head close to her ear. "Be very careful with this book."

She sipped her tea and continued reading.

Mrs. Twiggs burst into the room, ran up to Abigail, and gave her a big hug. "Abigail, that was quite a night," she said. "I've dreamed of this all of my life. All my years of searching for magic, and it was right in front of me."

Abigail smiled.

"I'm here to help you and Terra any way I can. Let me show you something," Mrs. Twiggs said. She walked over to the corner where a tattered banker's box sat open. "I've brought up a box from the basement full of some very old books on spells and potions that I've collected over the years. They're in pretty bad shape. Mrs. Tangledwood is reading one now."

We both glanced at the beautiful dark-haired woman, the pages of the book flipping themselves as she read. I jumped onto the coffee table next to the box. They smelled the same as the one in Mrs. Tangledwood's hands. Mrs. Twiggs had no idea what force she could unleash from these pages. The Wiccans weren't ready to contain this power. Mrs. Twiggs pulled out each book carefully. Abigail examined the tattered leather bindings shredding from their spine like an exhumed skeleton.

"Abigail, tell Mrs. Twiggs to box up all these books and put them away for safekeeping. The ladies aren't ready for them yet," I told her.

Abigail did as I directed, and so did Mrs. Twiggs. She retrieved the book from Mrs. Tangledwood and placed it carefully on top of the others. Mrs. Twiggs closed and sealed the box. While Abigail carried it back downstairs, Mrs. Twiggs settled into the chair by the fire. I climbed onto her lap. She stroked my fur softly. I realized I was unconditionally purring at her touch. I felt more and more like a cat than a witch as of late. Pixel sat in Mrs. Tangledwood's lap, purring and biting her blouse. "Terra tells me we should have caution with these books, Beatrice. Do you want me to hold on to them until the others' powers are stronger?"

"No, Emma, Terra thought it would be best if we put them away for now."

With that, Mrs. Twiggs looked over at her old friend, well not so old anymore. I could see the sadness in her eyes. She had spent her life chasing magic only to have it land at her doorstep, but the door was locked to her. I purred even louder and rubbed my head against her. She smiled, melting the sadness away.

Abigail pulled up a wicker chair and joined us by the fire. "So what's next?"

"I will evaluate each one of the Wiccans to assess their strengths. I will show Mrs. Tangledwood and Mrs. Twiggs potions that will help in their training. And then we begin our circle."

"What's that?"

"A closed coven of nine. It's the most powerful force against black magic. By combining all our strengths, we will shield Asheville from whatever darkness is gathering."

"But there's only eight of us?" Mrs. Tangledwood asked.

"Let me worry about that," I told her.

"I have to go to the pawnshop." Abigail stood up.

I looked around the room. Pixel was sound asleep, his tail dangling temptingly in front of Tracker's nose. Tracker stood.

We left Pixel to his slumber and headed to the pawnshop. Tracker heeled next to Abigail as we walked as though she had trained him to do so, only stopping occasionally for a sniff or to pick up something delicious from the sidewalk to eat. His tailless behind wiggled as Abigail reached down and scratched him behind the ears. Not being much of a canine enthusiast, I still found myself liking this dog.

Tracker and I waited outside as Abigail went inside to retrieve her watch. Tracker sat quietly, watching, turning his eyes left and right as the day's shoppers passed us by. Occasionally one would stop to pet him, and Tracker would let out a low growl. They would retract their hand and walk away. From inside the store we could hear Abigail's conversation with the pawnshop owner. "What do you mean you sold it? I still have five days left on my loan."

"Honestly I didn't think you were coming back. Look at you. You're homeless. I thought maybe you spent the money on drugs."

"I've got the ticket right here. It says I have five days."

"That's too bad, isn't it?"

"You can't do that. That's mine."

"What are you going to do? Call the police? By the looks of you, I don't think you want to get the police involved."

Tracker snapped his head around. I could see Abigail reach over the counter and grab the man by the shirt. He slapped her hand away. Tracker grabbed the door handle, opened it and flew in. He leapt onto the counter and barked ferociously in the storeowner's face, baring his teeth. "Get him out of here. Get this dog out of here."

Abigail tried to pull Tracker off the counter, but he wouldn't budge. The man reached under the counter as I ran behind. I could see him reach for a gun. I climbed up his back and scratched both cheeks as deep as I could, drawing blood. He screamed, dropped the gun, and fell to the floor. Abigail kicked open the door with Tracker on her heels. Behind the counter, I saw Abigail's mother's pocket watch. I grabbed it and flew out the door behind Abigail and Tracker. We didn't stop until we got back to Mrs. Twiggs. Pixel was screaming. "Terra left Pixel. Terra gone, Terra gone." Mrs. Twiggs was trying to console him, but he would not have it.

When he saw me, he tackled me. I dropped the watch. We somersaulted like a wagon wheel across the dining room floor. "Bad Terra, bad Terra. Pixel scared. You no go without Pixel."

"It's okay. We're back. You were asleep. We didn't want to disturb you."

"Never, Terra, never," he said with a stern fat cat voice. I couldn't help but laugh and love him.

Mrs. Twiggs picked up the watch. She examined it closely. She took out a loupe and rubbed her finger on the back of the case. "This is an Ed Patrick." She turned the watch over in her hands. "London, late seventeenth century. It's very valuable. Where did you get this?"

Abigail grabbed it from Mrs. Twiggs as though she were a pickpocket. "It was my mother's. It's all I have left of my real parents." She flipped open the case. I jumped up on the table to examine it. The time was frozen at three o'clock.

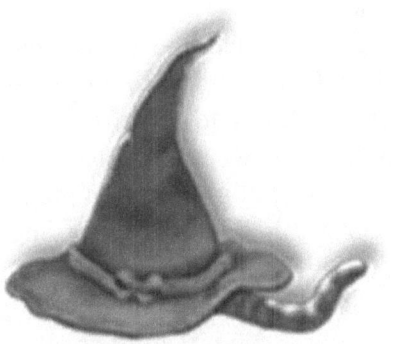

IN DREAMS, THEY COME

CAN'T BREATHE, MY LUNGS ARE filling with saltwater. My arms and legs splash frantically, trying to catch hold. I can't see through the murky water. I'm dying, I'm dying. A pinhole of light strikes me as the tide ebbs and flows out of the cave. I make it onto the rocks and collapse exhausted. It's still early morning, not enough light to give me away. I gaze down at my reflection in the tide pool, but it's not me. It can't be me. Elizabeth had said the vial would save my life, a chance for a new life but this isn't life. I'm neither witch nor human. I close my eyes in disbelief, but I can feel my new body. My soaking fur, my retractable claws, my tail. Heavens be, I have a tail. Elizabeth turned me into a cat. She, my friend, my mentor, how could she condemn me to this foul creature? Oh no. This is not a new life, this is a prison sentence. No, even worse than a prison sentence, a death sentence. She's killed my childhood. My chance to be a wife, a mother. I thought Elizabeth to be a friend. I must find her and make her turn me back. I hate you, Elizabeth. Can you hear me? I hate you. I will find you, I swear by our coven, I swear I will find you. I dragged myself across the beach, walking unevenly on my clumsy paws.

What are those sounds pouring into my ears? The woods are alive. Animals scurry, birds rattle, trees grow. I can hear everything. What torture has Elizabeth laid on me? Surely I will grow mad. I stop to rest in the hollow of a tree. The smell of the rodents makes my nose twitch, my stomach queasy. Or is that hunger? No, it cannot be hunger. I will not give in to this body. I will not lower myself to be a beast. I am Terra Rowan, descendant of a long line of white witches.

I walk along, gradually gaining confidence in my four paws. I continue into the village to find Elizabeth. I stop at the edge of the town where the tree line ends, thinking I have no need to hide. The village was, is, as it always was. Farmers pulling their produce in wagons, kids chasing behind, women preparing breakfast. I head toward Elizabeth's farmhouse and hear crying from within. I climb up to the windowsill to see Elizabeth's aunt sobbing at her table. She is holding Elizabeth's bonnet. I realize Elizabeth was in dire straits. She is the only one who could change me back. I must find her.

I continue down the road to the next farm. Constance will be helping her brother, gathering eggs or milking the cows. I make my way to the barn to see her brother sitting on a stool next to their cow, staring silently. No, not my dear Constance. They took Constance. The same fates unravel in front of me as I visit each of my coven sister's homes. The last home I reached was that of Prudence, the dearest of all my sisters. If I am to find refuge anywhere, it will be with her. She will accept me no matter what my fate. Before I could cross her fence, her dog appears, growling through the tall grass. I've played with this dog. He must know me. There must be some remnant of who I was that he should recognize. He inches closer, snarling. I say his name, but what comes out are nonsense noises. He lunges at the fence, snapping a wood board. I run as fast as I can on my four paws, crossing over the creek, slipping and falling, the fast-moving current almost pulling me down. For a moment I swear his eyes turned blood red as he stands on the other side, howling and barking. My fur is soaked and matted. I walk along the opposite bank. He stares before turning around and leaving.

I stare after him for a few minutes. I am cold and hungry and tired. The sun recedes into the pines. I shake from the cold. I have to eat. I have to eat something. Whatever it was to be won't be cooked. I will never eat a cooked meal again. Thankfully, I can smell everything. I can smell the late-blooming beach plums, the fragrant white spring flowers that I had danced through once now bear tart berries. I gather a feast. I breathe in the fox grape, another tart berry that offers sustenance. I am amazed to find the grapes I thought were so near are actually hundreds of feet from where I sit. My sense of smell is so intense. As I eat my way through the forest, I think I will survive at least for the night. I settle under an old ash tree. Why this tree? I do not know. I feel drawn to it. Maybe it is the vertigo that keeps my sense of direction from steadying, but something has led me to this tree. Even in the pitch-dark night I can look up from the trunk of the tree and see all the night creatures coming out. I feel safe here. This is the tree. When I was to turn eighteen years on October 31, this would have been my wanding tree. For tonight, it will suffice to be my bed.

"Terra, why you talk funny?" Pixel asked.

"What? What are you saying?" The dark and misty dream flew quickly out of my head like a murder of crows. "Pixel, I was dreaming."

"I saw dream. Pixel see dream," he said.

"You can see my dreams, Pixel?"

"Me familiar. Terra, come. Abigail, make food." Pixel danced excitedly around me, nudging me.

I could smell the back bacon and the biscuits from the oven. It smelled better than Abigail's usual fare. I followed Pixel into the tiny kitchen of the cabin. Mrs. Tangledwood had donned an apron and was pulling a tray of biscuits out of the wood stove. Out of all the Wiccans I had encountered both when I walked on two feet and now on four, I had never seen such rejuvenation. Not just of her physical outward beauty but her aura colors were brilliant, almost blinding to look at. Of all the ladies of the Biltmore Society, Emma Tangledwood would be the one to turn the tide of what would come.

I jumped up on the table and sniffed the fresh biscuits, a habit I had both as a young woman and a cat. Mrs. Tangledwood smiled and rubbed my back. I arched it uncontrollably. "Terra, it will take some time for me to get used to you. To get used to all the changes," she said. "Shall we eat breakfast and have a talk?"

Abigail poured the tea. I had gotten used to smelling the fresh honey she gathered and the nettle leaf. In her own way Abigail was trying to protect us, but she was not the ninth we needed to close our coven. On my journeys across the country, I had come across many different types of magic—Wiccans, shape shifters, wood nymphs—but never a witch. I was afraid that I was the last. I had seen Elizabeth hang, and although that took her flesh, her spirit had survived. I wandered in search of any sign of her. I spent decades, no centuries, searching for Elizabeth's daughter and the honorable Jonathan Goodall, Jr., who had disappeared from Salem after Elizabeth was executed. He had never returned, not even upon his father's death. I, too, never returned to Salem after Elizabeth. I could not stand by and watch the rest of my sisters be extinguished. Like Elizabeth's spirit, I am afraid they too left this world. Otherwise, surely we would have found each other in one form or another. That would have to wait until another day. The problem at hand is to find the ninth Wiccan and summon what powers she has. For this purpose I must count on Mrs. Tangledwood. She will be my apprentice.

"Terra dear, aren't you going to eat?" Mrs. Tangledwood asked, breaking my thoughts.

"Yes, Mrs. Tangledwood, of course. It smells delicious."

Pixel had already finished his third piece of bacon. Tracker was begging for his fifth. Abigail sipped the tea and stared quietly at me.

As Mrs. Tangledwood cleared the breakfast dishes, I walked outside with Abigail. She sat on the logs by the fire pit while I paced back and forth. Finally she broke the silence. "Are you going to tell me what's been on your mind?" She pulled her knife out of her boot. She flipped the blade into the ground, retrieved it and repeated it several times. I had noticed she did this when she was upset or nervous.

"Lionel and Bryson were watchers." I did not know how to explain to her what that meant. "Abigail, they were tasked to keep you safe."

"Why me? Why them?"

"That I don't know."

Abigail said, "Why would somebody want to kill them?"

I paused. "Lionel's life and yours are on a path leading to a crossroads. The black magic killed Lionel and Bryson because you are close to that crossroads."

Abigail stuck the knife back in her boot. "Terra, I can't do this. People are dying around me. I can't help you. This is insane. I'm heading back to Chicago."

"No, Abigail, no go." Pixel jumped out of the corner and onto Abigail. He put his paws on her chest and opened his saucer eyes wide. "No go, no go, no go," he said, kneading her.

Abigail cracked a smile. "Pixel, you'll be fine. You have Tracker and Terra and the nice ladies of the Biltmore Society."

"No, Abigail, no go," Pixel repeated. And then he spoke clearly with purpose and with an intelligence I had not thought possible. "No, Abigail, the storm is coming for you. Lionel tried to stop it." Pixel closed his eyes. "Terra?"

"Yes, Pixel."

"Pixel scared."

THE FILLMORE HOTEL

I WAITED UNTIL MORNING TO BRING my friends to the Fillmore. As of late, I didn't feel safe traveling at night. Dark things prefer dark places. It seemed that some myths are based on reality. The boogiemen, the noise in your closet, the shadow in the corner of your bedroom, are all monsters peering in at you through the window of an alternate world. Most humans can't see them, but they can feel them by the raised hair on the back of their neck, the goose bumps on their arms, the sensation of cold drafts, a creaky door, a loose floorboard, a movement out of the corner of your eye. Most of those creatures are not maleficent. Most are lonely souls, but there are the others who feed off sorrow and fear. Those creatures live in the realm of black magic. Elizabeth once told me that shining a light on the bumps in the night would make them take flight. I was only three at the time, so I thought it was a pretty bedtime story. After so many years of wandering the earth, I understood what she meant. Shining a light on black magic reveals its true identity and drains it of its power.

Abigail had filled her backpack with all her belongings. I had convinced her to make one stop before leaving town. Pixel and Tracker followed behind us. The streets were mostly empty. Anyone at dawn was either ending a long night or starting a long day. We arrived at the brass doors of the hotel where Wesley stood guard. Even when there were no guests to attend, Wesley never left his post. "Good morning, miss, I'm surprised to see you so early," he said. "You must be hungry."

"No thank you, Wesley. You're quite kind. I've come for a different purpose," I said.

"Terra, how come he can understand you?" Abigail asked. The constant beep of a cement truck coming down the alley distracted me. I could tell Wesley was annoyed by the commotion as well.

I hushed Abigail. "Quiet, Abigail."

"And who is this young lady?"

"I'm Abigail. Nice to meet you." She paused. "Wesley."

"It's a pleasure to make your acquaintance, Miss Abigail. You must excuse me, but breakfast will be served shortly. Guests will be waiting."

"Of course, Wesley." I interrupted. "You must be very busy getting ready for the opening tonight."

"Yes, we are expecting so many guests. And Mr. Vanderbilt will be here with the family." Abigail started speaking, but I shushed her, and Wesley continued in a whisper. "A very special guest from Louisiana, a medium, will be holding a séance. You know how the Vanderbilts enjoy a good séance." Wesley's face went blank. His coal-black eyes turned milky white in a moment, then he was back. "I'm sorry, young miss, you were saying?" Wesley reached under his sleeve and rubbed his arm, revealing the burn marks. "Yes, the séance is tonight. Mademoiselle gave me quite a list."

"What list, Wesley?" I asked.

"The strangest things: twigs of ash, oak, and thorn, nettle leaves."

Abigail turned pale.

"Thank you, Wesley," I said. We walked down the sidewalk, but Abigail kept turning her head to stare at the hotel.

"The hotel looks like it's been boarded over for years. What is Wesley doing here during all this construction?"

"It burned down years ago, but it was really something when it opened. That was the night I met Wesley." I closed my eyes and pictured the magnificent grand opening. I could hear the music. It was spring; I could smell the lilacs in bloom around me. Wesley was dapper in his livery.

"When did it burn down?" Abigail asked, interrupting my memories.

"The night it opened. George Vanderbilt built the hotel so his friends could stay here while the estate was being built."

Abigail quietly absorbed what I said and then broke in. "Wait a minute, Terra, that would make Wesley one hundred fifty years old."

"No, that would make Wesley what you would call a ghost. The night of the grand opening there was a great fire. Wesley relives that night every night."

I could hear Abigail's flesh crawling, the hair on the back of her neck stiffening, her heart pounding rapidly, her eyes dilating. "Why did you bring me here? I told you I couldn't help you."

"Abigail, I brought you here to show you that magic—good and bad—is everywhere. Running home to Chicago won't save you. The reckoning follows you wherever you go. It has you marked for some fate. Powers brought you to Asheville and brought others here to help protect you. Lionel couldn't but I can."

"Pixel too. Me protect Abigail," Pixel said.

Tracker barked and circled Abigail, gazing up at her with his ghost blue eyes. "Once we find the ninth Wiccan and close the coven, each of them will protect you too. This is where you need to be, Abigail."

"Who is this medium that Wesley was talking about?"

"This is the first time he's ever spoken of her. He was telling you not me, Abigail. Someone wanted you to know. We need to find out who she was."

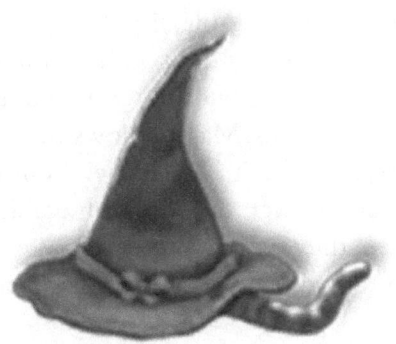

BILTMORE FOREST

B ILTMORE FOREST IS A COMMUNITY of exquisite homes and exclusive lifestyles. Tucked into a corner carved out of the woods surrounding the Biltmore Estate, it was its own little enclave. I walked these trails for many years. Like the woods I grew up in, this forest holds many mysteries. Some of the trees have stood here for hundreds of years, others were uprooted from foreign continents at the command of a scion, an heir to the throne of a railroad tycoon's fortune. George Vanderbilt carved his island into the North Carolina dirt to reap the rejuvenating benefits of the mountain air. His master landscape engineer Frederick Law Olmsted built his new world out of pieces of the old world, bamboo trees from the Orient, walnut from the Black Forest. Each turn of the path brought a new vista of Olmsted's vision. He was an alchemist, experimenting with different flora and fauna. I had slept many nights out in these woods, listening to the trees.

I led Abigail over to a rowan tree that had provided me shelter over many nights. Flashes of the crescent moon filtered through its bony branches. I rubbed my scent against the tree. Pixel did the same. Tracker ran off, chasing a squirrel. "This is my family tree, Abigail. The mountain ash," I said. "Using the term family tree to trace your heritage began with the Druids back in Ireland. They worshipped all the trees especially the oak. Families tethered their lives to their family tree. I feel most at home with the ash."

"Pixel like." He purred loudly, rubbing against the tree again.

"Me family tree too."

Abigail sat down under the tree. Pixel sat in her lap, arching his back as she stroked his fur. Abigail pulled a silver knife out of her backpack, studying it. "Why did you have me bring this, Terra?"

"Elizabeth warned me about testing such unproven magic. Black magic will be drawn to us. Magic knows magic. If evil does come, we must be prepared for it," I told her. "Until we discover each individual Wiccan's power, they are vulnerable, but once they are united as a coven, they will be protected."

"There's only eight, but you told me you need nine to have a closed coven?"

"I sense there's another Wiccan in Asheville. I haven't found her yet. Until I do, we need to prepare the rest," I said.

Before I could finish, we heard Tracker barking ferociously. He was standing behind Abigail, staring into the dark. Pixel ran up to Tracker's side and growled, puffing himself up. Even with my cat's eyes, I couldn't see into the blue black of the unlit forest. The canopy overhead strangled out any moonlight, but like Tracker and Pixel I could smell the pungent, malignant creature. The smell of death. Tracker began to charge into the deep woods. Abigail grabbed him, holding him close. He strained against her, growling. "No, Tracker, no," she cried out. And then the smell was gone.

We rose and took to the path again on our way to Mrs. Tangledwood's house. It rose up from the long driveway, a brick-and-stucco French chateau style, inspired by the Biltmore Estate. The crescent moon reappeared over the top of the peaked gables. I counted six not seven. I wondered if Mrs. Tangledwood was aware she was one gable short. Abigail stood and marveled at the decadence that old money provided. "Does she live here by herself?" she whispered.

I didn't answer. Abigail glanced at her torn jeans and worn leather jacket. Pixel cleaned his fur to make himself presentable. We stepped up to the ten-foot-high, hand-carved wooden door that had previously kept guard at the entrance of a thirteenth-century French monastery. Abigail knocked tentatively. A young servant woman opened the door and led us back toward the conservatory. The ladies were chattering away, sipping tea. I smelled several varieties but no nettle leaves. I could tell Abigail noticed also.

"Abigail dear, you made it. I don't know why you wouldn't let me send a car for you." Mrs. Tangledwood hugged Abigail, the diamond eternity necklace radiating in the moonlight. Her Jimmy Choos clicked on the marble entryway as she led us in. I noticed how far Mrs. Tangledwood had come since her awakening. She stopped by a vase of wilted roses and touched each stem, bringing them back to life. She smiled at me. Indeed, her powers of rejuvenation had grown since I had last seen her. Tonight, I'd learn her bloodline and the powers that gave her that ability.

"Terra wanted to show me some of the surrounding woods," Abigail said.

"Yes, of course, I'm glad you're here now. Have a cup of tea and some petit fours. Cook just took them out of the oven." Mrs. Tangledwood waved toward a small round table where we saw the elaborate trays of refreshments.

Pixel glanced at me for approval. I nodded my okay. He ran over to Mrs. Twiggs, jumped in her lap, and begged for a bite of her raspberry macaroon. Abigail walked to the blazing fire. From her backpack, she retrieved the eight bundles of twigs we had collected as we walked through the Biltmore Forest. I walked up next to her and turned to the ladies who were still chattering.

"Ladies, ladies, please," I said. They all stopped with their teacups midair and glanced down at me. Abigail placed the twigs by the fire. She closed the large French doors to the conservatory and switched the lights off. "Mrs. Stickman," I said, "please come up to the fire."

Mrs. Twiggs shifted on the velvet couch. "Oh dear, isn't someone going to explain to me what's going on?"

Abigail translated for me. "Terra says she is so sorry, Mrs. Twiggs." Abigail held up a bundle of twigs. "These are ash, oak, and thorn branches. They're tied with holly vines. According to Terra, it's the magical trinity of the witch world. The holly vine binds the three to make them stronger just as combining the ladies of the Biltmore Society will make you stronger. She wants each one of you to stand by the fire as we burn a bundle of the twigs. The smoke will engulf you. This will allow Terra to see your true light, the aura that surrounds all souls."

"I've read about similar ceremonies from many cultures that burn wood or incense. The Cherokee use birch to draw out bad spirits from their hunting grounds, Buddhist monks burn certain tea leaves, and early Appalachian settlers burned sage in the corners of the house to drive away bad spirits and bless their dwelling," Mrs. Twiggs said, nodding her understanding.

After Mrs. Stickman threw her bundle into the fire, she waited. The twigs crackled, a plume of smoke rose from the fire and surrounded her. Her body lifted off the floor. She froze suspended a foot off the ground. I watched what the rest couldn't see. The symphony of lights that danced around Mrs. Stickman. And then like the last seconds before death I could see Mrs. Stickman's life story pass before me. Her years at boarding school, her nanny reading to her in a rocking chair, her birth, her cells forming into an embryo, her spirit racing along a string of DNA back to the beginning of her families' bloodline. Before me stood not Mrs. Stickman but the good pagan witch of ancient Nigeria, Oya, goddess of violent storms. In the ancient years, the humans believed powerful witches were gods. Her colors were storm-cloud gray and lightning yellow white. Mrs. Stickman floated back to the floor, landing on her tiptoes softly. She woke out of her trance, shaking her head and staring intently at me. "I have the power to control the weather?" she asked.

"Your ancestor witches could summon a storm or two, but I'm afraid your bloodline has mingled for so many centuries with humans that it's weakened your ability. With practice you'll be able to summon some of those powers. Now that I know your strength I can help you," I said.

I continued with each lady. "Mrs. Jean Branchworthy, throw the bundle into the fire." As with Doris Stickman, Mrs. Branchworthy was engulfed with white smoke. She hovered in front of me, her eyes rolling back into her head, revealing Celtic fire. Her true light of red and yellow embers radiated around her. "Welcome child of Aodh," I said.

Mrs. Branchworthy smiled. "She was the Celtic witch goddess of fire."

I nodded my head. Mrs. Branchworthy sat back down. I called up Mrs. Bartlett. She stopped and turned to Mrs. Tangledwood, who urged, "Go ahead, dear." She urged her. "It'll be okay."

Mrs. Bartlett forced a smile. She reached for a bundle of sticks and then dropped them before running out of the room. Mrs. Tangledwood and I chased after her. We found her sitting in the throne chair, which stood guard in the entryway. Her face was buried in her hands.

Mrs. Tangledwood put her arm around her. "Nupur, dear, are you okay?"

Nupur lifted her head; tears stained her face. "Emma, I can't do this. This is too much, and I'm so very frightened."

"Nupur, we need you. I need you."

"You don't understand, Emma. When my family came to America, my parents wanted to assimilate into the American culture. They shunned the Hindu religion and our culture. They wanted to be Americans. They made me American. I cannot accept this mysticism, this so-called magic."

I rubbed up against her. I could feel her trembling. I sang to her in Hindu. She smiled. "My grandmother sang that song to me when I was a little girl in Delhi."

I leapt onto her lap and put my paws on her shoulder, whispering, "You have more strength and courage than you know, navasi." It was the Hindi word for daughter's daughter.

She smiled and hugged me. "I can do this," she said. We returned to the conservatory. Mrs. Bartlett stood in front of the fire, drew in a deep breath and threw her bundle of twigs into the blaze. Moments later, the smoke lifted her off the ground. I heard the temple bells chime. Kali, the goddess of time, creation, destruction and power, floated before me. Her radiant blue-and-gold aura emitted intense power. Kali, the destroyer of evil, the protector of good. Mrs. Bartlett awoke from her trance. She quietly sat down by the others.

I turned to the next. "Caroline Bowers, please come up." As Mrs. Bowers placed her bundle in the fire, I heard the faint resonance of the electric guitar. I hummed the melody to myself unable to keep from smiling as I sang along with Stevie Nicks to "Rhiannon," the Celtic goddess of the moon. Her colors were silver and black.

"I heard it too," Mrs. Bowers said, opening her eyes. "What powers does the moon hold?"

"In good time," I told her. "Please sit with the others." Then I turned back to them. "Mrs. Raintree, please," I said, following her up to the fire.

She stood straight and tall, the yellow glow of the flames highlighted her blue-black straight hair and her dark skin. I was reminded of Agatha Hollows and the nights we sat before her fire.

Mrs. Raintree emitted coral and turquoise, the colors of Elihino, the Cherokee goddess of the earth, a witch princess who ensured good harvest.

Next was Mrs. Loblolly. She shuffled to the hearth. Within moments after placing the twigs in the flame, I could smell the salt air. I could hear the flapping of the tall sails. The very large Mrs. Loblolly floated naked. Her long reddish-brown hair wrapped around the body of the Nordic goddess, Freya, the goddess of fertility and war. Her colors were sea mist green and the pale white of Valkyrie horns.

Gwendolyn Birchbark bowed politely to Mrs. Tangledwood before standing in front of the fire. She placed her bundle in and awaited her revelation. Kuan Yin, the Chinese goddess of mercy and compassion, a very ancient goddess who some believed was one of the very first white witches to have walked the earth. Her aura shone red and sun yellow.

The ladies talked over each other in their excitement as they shared what they had seen. I watched Mrs. Twiggs as each of her friends began their new life. I felt sad I couldn't help her.

Mrs. Stickman pulled her ponytail, raven hair, from behind her neck to study the streak of white. The ladies looked at each other; they each bore the same streak. "What's with the streak of white?"

"Now you begin your journey to become a coven," I said.

There was a tap at the French doors. The maid entered, carrying a tray with champagne flutes. After taking one, the ladies toasted each other.

"Emma, you have not burned your bundle," Mrs. Twiggs said.

"Yes, of course." She put her champagne flute down and stepped over to the fire. Tracker let out a low growl and ran to the long window. As she went to put her bundle into the fire, a gust of wind came down the chimney, tossing ash and embers around the room. Smoke poured out of the fireplace, choking the air. The ladies screamed and darted out onto the lawn. A spark caught the velvet couch, which ignited instantly followed by the drapes. Mrs. Tangledwood fell onto the lawn, choking. All around me the ladies of the Biltmore Society coughed and gasped for air. In the distance, we could hear the scream of the fire trucks. After recovering, Mrs. Tangledwood lifted me off the ground. "What is it? What is happening?"

"We've summoned the black magic." My words hung in the air as we breathed in the dark smoke.

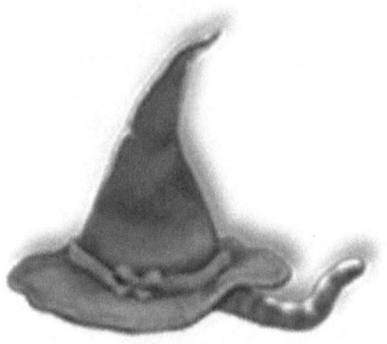

JEAN BRANCHWORTHY

"**M**RS. BRANCHWORTHY," I SAID.

"Please, Terra, I've asked you to call me Jean," she replied.

Mrs. Branchworthy, Jean, sat on her screen porch, snapping her fingers. As she did, small puffs of smoke appeared. Abigail and Mrs. Twiggs sat down in the white wicker chairs across from Mrs. Branchworthy and me.

"Oh, where are my manners? Can I get anyone some tea? I'll have my maid prepare some."

"Oh, no thank you, Jean," Mrs. Twiggs said politely.

I leapt onto the small coffee table. I could see Pixel and Tracker running in the backyard. Mrs. Branchworthy's house was much less grand than Emma Tangledwood's. Not much more than a large turn-of-the-century farmhouse that she and her husband had been restoring for the past several decades. Mrs. Twiggs had told me the history of the Branchworthy farm, one of the last remaining ten-acre farmettes in Biltmore Forest. Each acre could sell for over a million dollars to build a ten-thousand-square-foot monstrosity. The Branchworthys felt it important to maintain the green space as they called it of their small community. Now almost sixty years later, Jean's children and her grandchildren had grown and moved out, scattered across the country. Mrs. Twiggs told me that at times Jean felt left behind. After her husband died, the children barely made it home for a birthday or Christmas. Jean had dedicated her life to her husband and her children and caring for her home. I do not like the term homemaker. It seems to diminish the importance of a woman who raises a family. She was a care-giver, a teacher, and a mentor.

I watched Jean snapping both fingers. "May I ask what you are doing, Jean?"

"I'm summoning fire," she said, gazing at me.

"I see. I think before we attempt that, you should understand the history of your bloodline."

"Oh, of course. My grandparents came from Cork in Ireland during the potato famine. They settled in New York."

I interrupted. "Jean, I mean to go a bit farther back."

"Oh, okay."

"You are a descendant of the Celtic fire goddess, Aodh. She was a very powerful white witch who could summon fire. The fables tell of her hurling fireballs at the invading Romans. My mentor, Elizabeth, told me that Aodh understood the alchemy of harvest-ing the powers of the sun through her fingertips."

Jean stopped snapping her fingers with a horrified look.

"Oh, no, Jean, you won't be able to wield that power, but with enough practice and understanding the physics behind your power, you shall be a formidable force," I told her.

"I don't understand, Terra. Do I just think it and it happens? I've been practicing all morning. I picture fire, I can feel the heat in my fingertips, but nothing comes out except small puffs of smoke."

I leapt up next to Jean on the couch. I looked around and spot-ted my reflection on the antique mirror leaning against a potted plant. "Jean, come with me." I led her to the mirror. Jean stood in front of it, turning left to right then looking over her shoulder.

"I look thirty again and thin."

"Do you believe the image in the mirror, Jean?"

"Yes, of course, I'm looking right at my reflection."

"The image you see is what your mind portrays you as. This is your true self, your true light. This is as Aodh perceived herself and all her descendants. Because you believe it, it is true. The same is true for your powers. You must believe that you can summon fire. It must be as sure to you as the sun will rise tomorrow or the stars will shine tonight. You must believe that it is part of the physics of nature. Believe it and it shall be true."

"Terra, I feel the heat rising from my body to my fingertips."

"Stop thinking, Jean; empty your mind. Do you need to think to breathe?"

"No, I just breathe."

"It's mechanical. The same is true of your powers."

As we spoke, small flames rose from Jean's fingertips. She raised her hands and stared with a delighted smile.

"It begins, Jean."

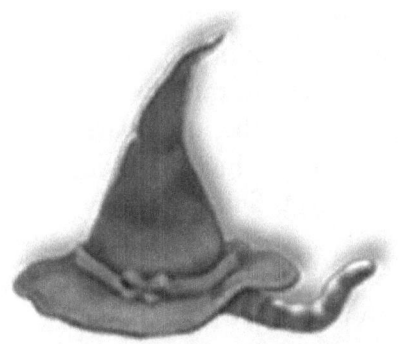

DORIS STICKMAN

"THE GODDESS OYA CONTROLLED WINDS and storms. She ruled over Nigeria and before that the fertile crescent where mankind began," I told her. "Her bloodline and yours goes back much farther than humans."

"Terra, my ancestors were slaves. They were brought here in the 1700s. My grandfather four times removed was a slave here in North Carolina until the emancipation. He helped the freed slaves settle on the land at the Biltmore Estate," Mrs. Stickman said.

"That's on your father's side of the family. Wiccans carry their mothers' bloodline."

"Like most descendants of slaves, there is not much official documentation about my family before the Civil War."

"When you threw your sticks into the fire, Oya appeared to me. You are her descendant."

Mrs. Stickman rubbed her pointy chin. Her great-grandchildren ran in from the backyard, jumping on her lap. "Nana, why do you look so good?" the youngest asked.

Mrs. Stickman smiled and rubbed the young boy's head. "Y'all go back outside now. I have business with Mrs. Twiggs."

Mrs. Twiggs smiled at the children as they ran back outside. We could hear their laughter as they played. We sat in Doris's library. When we had arrived, I admired her collection of first editions, most of them written by African-American authors, including an original diary written by abolitionist Harriet Tubman. She had caught me glancing at it. She had told me her great-grandfather was an acquaintance of Ms. Tubman. Her early-twentieth-century, Craftsman-style home was small compared to the other ladies, but it was well built and comfortable. Her home stood on the land that was originally given to the freed slaves by George Vanderbilt.

Earlier, as we drove up the long gravel driveway to her house, I had seen many slaves walking the open meadow, carrying sickles on their way to the crop fields. I was the only one who saw them.

"Terra, how do I begin?" Mrs. Stickman asked.

"There is a barometer within all of us. Do you ever feel you can tell when a storm is approaching?"

She thought for a moment before replying, "My arthritis acts up if a cold front is coming. My sinuses bother me right before a rainstorm."

"Your body is in tune with these changes in the atmosphere. Think of yourself like a lightning rod reacting to the atmosphere around you. This is a symbiotic relationship. As the weather affects you, you too can affect the weather. Have you ever felt gloomy or sad on a rainy day?"

"Yes, I think many people do."

I thought for a minute. This was a lot to convey to her. "Doris, I'd like you to think of something sad right now. Would you please?"

Doris nodded her head and closed her eyes. As she did I ran to the window. Nothing. It was a beautiful sunny day.

"Doris, what were you thinking about?"

"I was thinking about the other night at Mrs. Tangledwood's and the fire."

"No, Doris, think of something that touches you deeply. Something very personal." As I spoke, Doris turned her eyes to the framed picture of her and husband's wedding photo. Her husband has passed years before. She picked it up and sat behind the desk. She closed her eyes. Behind her, the large palladium window began to ping from drops of rain. Storm clouds gathered. She began to cry. The clouds opened up, and a torrential rain came down upon the house. She opened her eyes, and just as quickly the storm clouds disappeared and the sun peeked through. She looked at me with disbelief. "You need to learn to calibrate those emotions so you can control them."

"How do I do that?"

I ran over to Mrs. Twiggs who opened her purse and handed me a pigeon feather. I took it in my mouth and then leapt onto the desk in front of Mrs. Stickman and dropped it. She picked it up and stared. "Think about your husband and then blow gently on this feather." As she did, I could see some leaves rustle in the window. "Now, Doris, blow hard."

As she did, pebbles flew against the window. "That's enough for now," I said. Her smile lit up her face. "Concentrate your emotions and picture the elements. And then you will be able to control them."

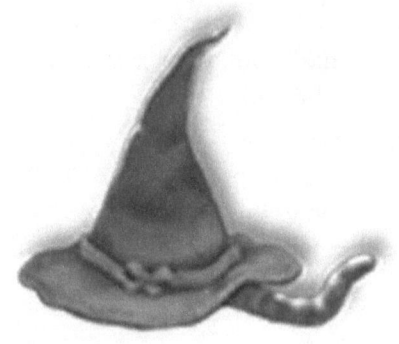

NUPUR BARTLETT

I COULD SMELL THE CURRY AS Nupur hurried herself about her kitchen. She insisted on making a special meal for us before beginning her training. Pixel was very excited. He had never tasted East Indian food. Abigail and Mrs. Twiggs sat at the dining room table, talking softly as Nupur bustled around the kitchen.

"Me hungry," Pixel said.

"Don't be rude, Pixel," I told him.

"Mrs. Bartlett is so quiet and reserved. How are you going to make her a slayer of demons?" Abigail asked.

"It's in her blood. She needs to build her confidence. Quiet, here she comes."

Nupur backed out of the kitchen though the swinging doors, carrying a tray filled with steaming Indian food. "I have prepared chicken curry, jasmine rice and nanna." I could hear Pixel's tail thumping under the table. Tracker sat quietly by Abigail's feet.

Mrs. Bartlett hesitated before allowing the animals into her home. Her beautiful five-thousand-square-foot colonial was located on the southeast corner of Biltmore Forest, and was surrounded by lovely gardens. Mrs. Bartlett's late husband was renowned for his roses. He had served in the Carolina senate for nearly forty years and like many men of his age had passed, shortly after retirement.

Mrs. Bartlett served the food. Abigail placed bowls under the table for us "animals." I suddenly felt ridiculous, eating Far Eastern Indian food off fine china under a table next to Pixel who was grunting and slopping food everywhere and Tracker who was licking his bowl clean. I finished eating and wandered throughout the house, leaving their conversation behind me. I stopped to admire an Atul Dodiya painting, *Woman from Kabul*, an Indian modernist master reinterpreted. I stood transfixed. I had seen similar paintings in the Biltmore. I rubbed my head against the gold leaf wallpaper which could be seen as garish yet somehow fit the great room. I glanced back at my comrades sitting around the Henredon table, overhead a Swarovski crystal chandelier. Mrs. Bartlett had made a lovely home for her family. It made me sad to think I would never have a home like this and even sadder that I would never have a family.

I tiptoed back into the dining room and climbed up on a chair next to Mrs. Bartlett. "Please Terra, please call me Nupur."

"Of course, Nupur. Lunch was delicious. Thank you."

"Of course, you're most welcome. I know the myth about Kali. My grandmother would tell me stories when I was a little girl. But when we came to America, my father forbid her from speaking of the old county."

"I understand."

"My grandmother believed she had special powers. She would light candles and pray to Kali and her wishes would often come true."

"Your witch bloodline goes back through the females of your family even as the women of your family married and their surnames changed. Their heritage followed them. Your name Bartlett from the pear tree is a derivative of your ancient name."

"I don't understand. I married Joseph Bartlett, and he was American. His family was originally Scotch-Irish."

"Magic knows magic. Even though he was human, somewhere there were witches in his family perhaps back in Ireland or Scotland. Wiccans find their tree name whether through marriage or through their maternal bloodlines. Your husband's family's magic dwindled though the years, yet you were still drawn to it."

"Shall we adjourn to the sitting room?" Nupur stood up from the table and led us into the adjoining living room, decorated with antiques. I was surprised to see a gold statue of Kali sitting on top of a cabinet. "This was my grandmother's. I had stored it away for years. I brought it out from the attic after the ceremony."

Abigail examined the statue closely. "My grandmother would pray to Kali to protect us, to watch over us and keep us from evil. She told me that Kali would speak to her in dreams. She told me of one dream she had of me as a young woman dressed in my wedding sari astride an elephant. I was brandishing a sword and slashing at thousands of crows that flew down upon me," recalled Mrs. Bartlett.

"Nupur, you shall be our protector. The black magic fears you. It knows the power you could wield, but you must believe in yourself." At my nod, Abigail pulled a knife out of her boot.

The twelve-inch-long silver blade glowed white-hot as Nupur touched its handle. "Abigail is quite good with knives. She is going to teach you how to wield it. With practice, your confidence will grow."

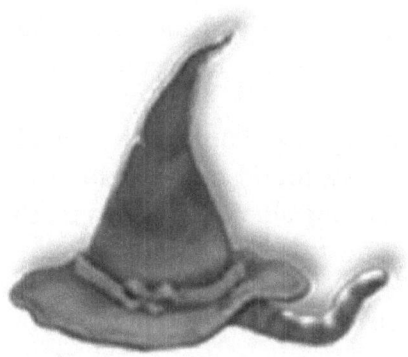

GWENDOLYN BIRCHBARK

NEXT ON MY LIST WAS Gwendolyn Birchbark. Mrs. Twiggs drove along Creek Road, which ran the perimeter of the Biltmore Forest community. After leaving Nupur Bartlett's house, I began to see a pattern I had not noticed before. I had Abigail Google map all the ladies' houses for me. She turned around in her seat in the front of the car and held up her iPhone. "You were right, Terra, look," she said.

The little red dots on the Google map formed a perfect circle. Without knowing why, all the ladies lived in homes, which formed a circle on the perimeter of Biltmore Forest as if they had already known they were a coven. Each keeping watch, protecting something deep within the forest. Something drew them to these woods and to each other. A crossroads of white magic bloodlines from around the world. We reached Mrs. Birchbark's home, a Victorian. I had read her house was on the national registry and was originally owned by Olmsted's apprentice and master arborist, Wendell Waxman.

Mrs. Twiggs from over her shoulder asked, "Terra, what's going on?"

Abigail related the coincidence of the mapping of the ladies' homes.

"Mm, that's interesting," she said.

Tracker and Pixel led the way up the circle driveway to the wraparound porch, which was decorated with scarecrows and pumpkins and cornstalks. Abigail avoided the scarecrows. Mrs. Birchbark greeted us. "I thought it was such an unusually warm fall day we might sit on the front porch and talk," she said. "I've made sweet tea." She pointed to a small table at the far end of the porch.

Pixel and Tracker jumped up onto the small cedar love seat. Abigail and Mrs. Twiggs found two matching rocking chairs. I leapt onto the railing, facing all of them. Mrs. Birchbark poured tea and sat in the rocker next to Mrs. Twiggs.

"Gwendolyn, how did you find this beautiful house?"

Mrs. Birchbark placed her iced tea glass down on a side table. "My husband, Stanley, wanted to live in Weaverville, fifteen miles from here. He owned several building supply companies, but I was really drawn to Asheville and the woods. I loved the history of it, loved the trees." She spoke with a delicious Southern drawl; her words lingered a bit longer in the air as though not willing to be exhausted.

"I understand, but why this particular house?"

"We found it, now this was maybe thirty years ago? It was in dire need of repair. It had such charm and such history, I felt it worthy of the work. Of course my husband being a contractor did a lot of the work himself. For some of the masonry and fine carpentry, he used local artisans. I did a lot of research at the Asheville library." She drew a long pause. "I found some original photographs from when the house was built in 1890. I tried to be as true to the original construction as possible, you understand." She paused for a moment. "I couldn't think of moving after Stanley passed."

"I see," I said. "It's a beautiful home, and you've taken great care of it. Tell me more what drew you to Biltmore Forest."

"I believe there is a history here, and I don't mean to seem flippant, but you can feel the magic in the air."

Mrs. Twiggs smiled as Abigail translated our conversation.

"At night I open my windows and listen to the owls. The songbirds wake me at predawn. Even though I'm just a mile from Creek Road and the busy downtown, I feel like these woods are another world."

I walked along the long railing, admiring the soaring aspens and cedars. I spotted several owls' nests, a good sign that they watched over Mrs. Birchbark. Owls have always been friends to the witch, not familiars but equals in their own way. The Chinese witches brought owls with them as they walked over the earth. They were what we called the ancient earth walkers. Yes, this was a safe place.

"Terra."

I broke from my thoughts and walked back to where they all sat.

"I've been doing some reading about Kuan Yin, the Chinese goddess of mercy and compassion. My family dates back to the Chou dynasty. My great-grandfather came over from China to San Francisco during the railroad expansion. He became one of the first Chinese railroad engineers allowed to work on the Transunion Railroad. Eventually that's when he met Vanderbilt and was commissioned to help run the railroad into Biltmore Forest to bring supplies to build the estate." She paused. "I have many photographs and letters from my great-grandfather about those railroad days and even some from his mother from China that she wrote to him when he came to San Francisco. But I've never read or seen anything in our family history about Kuan Yin."

Mrs. Twiggs said, "Who is Kuan Yin?"

"Kuan Yin is one of the most revered goddesses in all of China. According to legend, she was about to enter paradise after achieving Nirvana when she heard cries from Earth. She rushed back to Earth to ease the suffering and achieved immortality."

"Terra, I don't understand. What powers does Mrs. Birchbark possess?" Mrs. Twiggs asked.

"Mrs. Birchbark has the most powerful magic to combat black magic. She has compassion. The way to defeat evil is through self-sacrifice and love. Her mother witch Kuan Yin gave up eternal paradise to ease the suffering of others. Mrs. Birchbark's mercy and compassion will cloak us through the dark days ahead."

"How do I do that? What kind of magic does it take to protect all my friends?" Mrs. Birchbark asked.

"You've already brought the magic to us." As I spoke, nine owls flew out from the tree lines and landed on the railings next to me. "Gwendolyn, send them to watch over your friends."

Mrs. Birchbark addressed herself to each owl in turn and whispered in their ears. As all but one flew off, she sat back down in her rocking chair and rocked slowly.

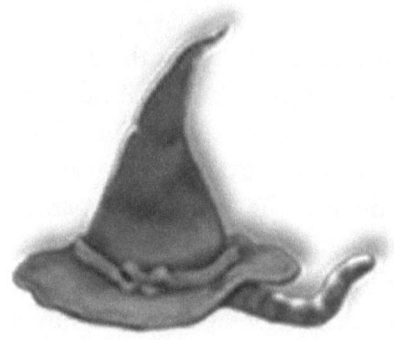

CAROLINE BOWERS

AS WE DROVE TO CAROLINE Bowers's estate, Mrs. Twiggs played the Fleetwood Mac self-titled album. The haunting melody of "Rhiannon" has played in my head since the night of Mrs. Bowers's reveal. Abigail tapped the dashboard in time to the drums. Mrs. Twiggs bobbed her head. Pixel and Tracker were oblivious. I had been backstage in 1975 when Fleetwood Mac played in Boston. I was living in Mystic at the time and heard about the show coming to Boston. I walked all night, sneaking past some roadies through the back door. I hid behind the Marshall amps and watched Stevie Nicks spinning on stage, her black lace chasing behind her. My heart pounded. She understood witches and what drove us. Her words spoke to me. At the end of the show, I couldn't help myself. I found my way to her dressing room just to be closer to her. She discovered me hiding in the shadows. She was the first creature to recognize me for who I am. Neither witch nor human. Stevie Nicks has powers through her music. It is an ethereal power that transcends this world.

Mrs. Bowers waited for us on the northeast corner of the woods. Our daylong journey to each of the ladies' houses had turned into evening. I had not yet quite understood how each of the ladies' powers were entwined with their home site. I thought about the children's book, *The Wizard of Oz*, and the witches of the four quadrants. L. Frank Baum stumbled upon a truth about witches. We are tied into geographic locations—the ladies to the Biltmore

Forest and their particular quadrant of the forest.

Mrs. Bowers's home dripped with kudzu entwined in elegantly carved wrought iron trellises. It reminded me of plantations I had seen in New Orleans. She led us to the back veranda so the moonlight could drip down on us, she said. I could hear the rush of water from the stream that ran along the back of her property. She understood the white magic of running water.

Her black-blue hair swung down her back, accenting the pale ivory of her freckled skin. Her eyes were clear and sapphire blue. Her flowing black lace gown clung to her slender frame. She floated toward us, twirling once in the moonlight. I couldn't help but be reminded of Stevie Nicks. I was the only one who could see both versions of Mrs. Bowers. Her inward beauty and her earthly wear. When the ladies looked in the mirror, they saw their inward beauty, but to those around them they appeared almost unchanged. They appeared as they should a woman of their age, perhaps more spry, a twinkle in their eye.

"Where do we begin?" Caroline trilled. The moonlight enhanced her newfound youthful glow. Her skin absorbed the moonlight like melatonin to sunlight. It charged her.

Abigail sat in a wrought iron lounge, bathing herself in the moonlight. She, too, had an affinity for the night. Her feet danced to the silent music that only she could hear through her earbuds.

Mrs. Twiggs rubbed her elbow.

"What's wrong?" Caroline asked.

"Oh, it feels like a cold front is coming. My arthritis."

Mrs. Bowers walked over and turned on the outdoor gas fireplace. Mrs. Twiggs settled next to the fire, wrapped in her shawl. As the Biltmore ladies felt younger, I feared Mrs. Twiggs was experiencing the opposite effect. The stress of recent events had drained her. For now, I needed to turn to the matter at hand.

Abigail translated for Mrs. Twiggs as I spoke. "Rhiannon means white witch or great queen." I curtseyed and bowed my head. "You have royal blood and possess the deepest magic of all," I continued.

Mrs. Bowers curtseyed back. "My family were poor farmers. My father from Ireland, my mother from Wales. I don't believe we have any royalty in our family, far from it. We were quite poor when we came to America. I married well. My husband, the colonel, was in the tobacco industry."

I thought to myself how all the ladies had outlived their husbands, not so unusual for women in their seventies and eighties.

Mrs. Bowers asked, "How can I help, Terra?"

"You, Caroline, are the thread that binds us. Your mother witch conjured great white magic. Rhiannon could manifest dreams and desires for the good of all kind. She used the forest fairies and nymphs to cast dreams and fulfill wishes upon the deserving." As I spoke, I could see the fireflies flickering through the woods, the tiny fairies that surrounded Caroline's estate. She could not see them yet or not allow herself to see them.

"Terra, how do I do that?"

"You do that through your dreams. You have the power to make dreams come true. You are our labyrinth of the unconscious. Reach out to each of your sisters tonight as you sleep, send out your magic in their slumber."

Mrs. Bowers smiled and filled a goblet full of wine. "I may need some inspiration for that." She drank it quickly and then filled it again.

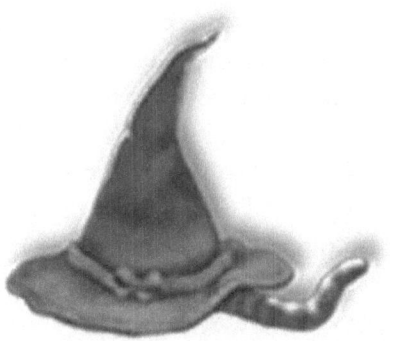

JUNE LOBLOLLY

JUNE LOBLOLLY TOUCHED THE GOLD necklace around her neck. Elaborate scrollwork was wrapped around amber cabochons.

"What a beautiful necklace," Mrs. Twiggs said.

"It's been in my family for generations. It was handed down to me by my mother who got it from her mother. It's always handed down to the oldest daughter."

"It does look ancient," Mrs. Twiggs said, admiring it.

I took a deep breath. From the kitchen I could smell the cardamom baking. All about her mansion, fresh flowers adorned nooks and crevices. The sweet fragrance of gardenias wafted through the air mixing with the cardamom spice. We followed her into the dining room. Mrs. Loblolly laid out a beautiful table for us adorned with crystal vases full of exotic flowers. We took our places. June brought in a tray of fresh-baked bread and jars of preserves. As she twisted a jar open, I smelled the lingonberries. Mrs. Loblolly was the Mrs. Fields of preserves. Unlike the other ladies in the Biltmore Society, June did not marry into a fortune. She built her own wealth through hard work and determination.

Mrs. Twiggs bit into the bread. "This is so good. I should sell this at my shop. Would you share the recipe?"

Mrs. Loblolly sat back in her chair, her gold bracelets dangling. "I'm afraid I can't share the recipe. It's an old family secret."

Abigail placed a plate full of bread and preserves on the floor for Tracker and Pixel. Pixel growled at Tracker, who jumped away from Pixel as he ate with an urgency, his whole body shuddering.

I stared at the necklace. I had seen an illustration of one similar in a book. "June, I'm sorry to obsess about the necklace, but I've never seen you wear it before," Mrs. Twiggs said.

"I've kept it in a safety deposit box, but as of late I felt the need to wear it," she said, touching the largest amber stone.

I remembered where I had seen the necklace. Elizabeth had a book of mythology. She had warned me that the lines between reality and mythology were blurred. This necklace belonged to the Norse goddess Freya who had sacrificed her love to obtain it. Odin had cursed her to walk the earth searching for her lost love. Her tears falling onto the earth turned to gold, and into the sea the tears became amber. The humans drew from pagan mythology, taking from it their own glimpses of the truth, but the actual truth was still sprinkled into the stories there for the finding. June's witch mother, Freya, appeared to me during her reveal. This was her necklace. June did not know the power that the necklace could wield. As with all the ladies, I'd dole out knowledge by the spoonful rather than by the cup.

"June, we have visited all your sisters but one," I said. "The coven has begun closing."

June dabbed at the jelly drop on her lips with her lace napkin. "How may I help?"

"Your blood once flowed through the Vikings. Your witch mother, Freya, was their guide to Valhalla."

"I know the history of the Vikings and the mythology."

"Yes, most are bedtime stories, but Freya was real. She was a powerful white witch of the north. In these dark days to come, we will need a guide to lead us. That is your power."

"I understand." She gave a knowing smile.

As Abigail relayed our conversation to Mrs. Twiggs, I could see Mrs. Twiggs nervously fidgeting in her chair. "Abigail, ask Mrs. Twiggs what's wrong?" I said.

As she did, Mrs. Twiggs turned to me. "Terra, I thought you told us that the ladies were all Wiccans and they had untapped white magic powers that would make an arsenal against the black magic. It seems like their powers are just emotional. Now you're saying June is going to be our guide. What does that mean?"

"Abigail, tell Mrs. Twiggs that all Wiccans have basic potion and spell casting powers. They have limited abilities to read minds, summon spirits. They can be taught with spell books and potion recipes, but there is a much deeper strength within them. All those powers flow from their true light. June's true light is that to guide whether it is from one world to the next or deciding a path of less resistance—it doesn't matter. The point is we are going to call on her when we question how to move forward."

Mrs. Twiggs stood and walked around the table. I could tell she was upset. My exact reason for doling out teaspoons of knowledge. Wiccans and humans have no idea of the powers that exist in the worlds and within themselves.

June reached up and grabbed Mrs. Twiggs's hand. "Beatrice, sit. This is a lot for all of us to take in. I'm sure Terra has a plan."

Mrs. Twiggs settled down, reaching for another slice of bread and slathering the preserves. She sighed.

At that moment, it struck me. "Abigail, which way did we drive to arrive here?"

Abigail thought for a moment. "North, I think."

I ran to the window and gazed out. Mrs. Loblolly's house was located true north on the coven's circle of homesites. True north, which is the direction we travel in times of uncertainty. All the Wiccans would meet here at Mrs. Loblolly's. They would be drawn to this home.

June reached into her apron pocket and retrieved a brass compass. She placed it on the table. "My grandmother gave this to me. She told me that, in times of trouble, head north."

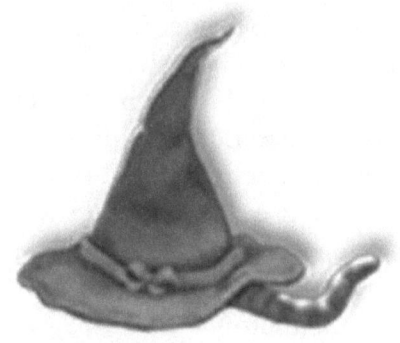

WANDA RAINTREE

I T WAS NEARLY NINE P.M. when we arrived at Wanda Rain-tree's home, an expansive log cabin overlooking the Biltmore Estate. My companions and I were exhausted, but the urgency to train the Wiccans drove us forward. Mrs. Twiggs fell asleep by the roaring fire. The interior of the massive cabin was decorated with Cherokee family heirlooms. On either side of the floor-to-ceiling stone fireplace were two ten-foot-tall windows, adorned with dream catchers. Agatha Hollows had made dream catchers for the mountain folk. Two versions, one to catch good dreams, the other to repel nightmares. I had noticed that both Mrs. Raintree's dream catchers were to ward away nightmares. This worried me.

Abigail looked over the collection of knives in a glass display case. "Those belonged to my husband," Wanda explained. "Much of these heirlooms were from his family. They were from Chero-kee. His grandfather was a shaman."

"How long have you been having nightmares?" I asked.

Abigail sat down in a chair next to Mrs. Twiggs. "How do you know she's having nightmares?"

Wanda glanced up at the dream catchers. "My husband placed those in the windows. There are more over our bed. My doctor says the nightmares are from the Ambien. I have trouble sleeping. I thought the dream catchers were silly, but he believed in them. The dreams have gotten worse recently."

"Tell me about them," I said, fighting the heaviness taking over my eyes.

Wanda closed her eyes, opened them, and poured herself a cup of coffee. I thought it strange for someone who had trouble sleeping to drink caffeine this late. She heard my thoughts. "As of late, I don't want to sleep. I don't want to dream." She settled on the couch next to me unconsciously rubbing her hand along my back. Tracker and Pixel fell asleep by the fire. "It begins the same. I'm walking through the woods. It's a beautiful spring day. I'm walking down a path. I suddenly realize I'm dressed in a tear dress."

"What's a tear dress?" Abigail whispered.

"It's a Cherokee dress made at the time when the Cherokee were forbidden scissors so they had to tear the material from larger pieces," Wanda said. "The path leads me into a large field with early spring corn. I reach down and touch a stalk. It grows over my head and fills with corn. As I walk along the rows, touching the tops of the stalks, they all grow. I look up at the sun as a dark cloud crosses over. It's not a cloud, it's crows. Thousands of crows descend onto the corn, tearing and ripping. Then they turn to me, tearing my dress, tearing the flesh off my bones, pecking at my eyes. I wake up screaming." Her coffee cup jingled on the top of the saucer as her hand shook.

Abigail sat down next to her and put her arm around her.

"Wanda, your witch mother is the goddess Elihino," I said.

Wanda looked up. "Yes, I know who she is. She is the earth mother, one of the sisters of the trinity. Her sister Sehu, the goddess of corn, and Igaehinvdo, the goddess of the sun. Eliniho accepts the seeds of corn and blesses the harvest. After my reveal, I realized what my nightmares were about. She was calling to me to protect the harvest from the black magic, to protect my sisters, but I don't know how."

"Lie down on the couch."

"Why?"

"Please just lie down."

Wanda did as I asked. I climbed up on the back of the couch, looking down on her. "I want you to sleep."

"I can't sleep. I don't want to sleep."

"Trust me, Wanda, your sisters will be there for you."

As Wanda closed her eyes, I sang to her the song Agatha Hollows sang to the Appalachian children when they had nightmares. "Let your thoughts drift softly on the midnight winds." As I sang, I saw the tension in her face release, her breathing slow. I called out to Caroline Bowers, and then I entered Wanda's dream. I watched her walking into the cornfield. From the other side of the field Caroline walked toward her. From each corner of the field came a Wiccan. Wanda stopped and stared up at the sky. Not a single crow flew overhead, but just one great horned owl circled. Wanda's eyes popped open, a smile on her face.

"I will teach you what herbs to plant around your sisters' homes, how to bless them. I will teach you all I've learned from Agatha Hollows who knew the Cherokee ways. Their power is great in these mountains. The tears they shed bless the ground we walk on now."

Wanda took me in her arms and hugged me, crying, tears pouring down her face.

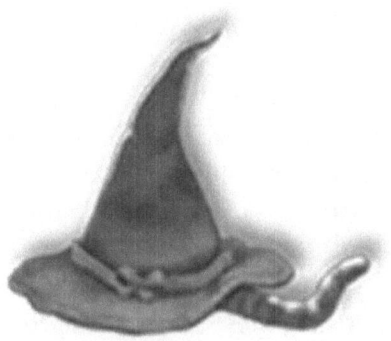

THE STUDY

COMPLETE DARKNESS. I CAN HEAR voices. I smelled the dusty tomes. Abigail was speaking to the curator inside the Biltmore Estate. Mrs. Twiggs had arranged for her to have access to George Vanderbilt's personal study where the curators kept the history of the estate, personal items of George Vanderbilt, his memoirs, and artifacts not typically seen by the public. As a volunteer, Mrs. Twiggs knew the staff at the estate, and much like the rest of Asheville had, they welcomed her into their community. Abigail thanked the young woman for allowing her into the library. I could hear the click of her sensible shoes on the parquet floor and the door closing behind her. Abigail opened the flap of her backpack. I jumped out onto an oak table.

"What are you looking for, Terra?"

"Anything we can find about the opening of the Fillmore, any memoirs, notes, books dating to the 1880s when Vanderbilt began building in Asheville. And the woman Wesley spoke of. Her life and that of the ladies of the Biltmore Society are tied to these woods." This was my first visit behind the velvet rope of the Biltmore. Although not as ornate as the rest of the house, this study still showcased the intricate detail of this magnificent estate. Mahogany shelves floor to ceiling encased the entire room, a spiral staircase stood in one corner, a Zulu wall mask hung on one wall next to a seventeenth-century bronze Buddha, each souvenirs from his travels. On his desk sat a cast-iron replica of his grandfather's first ship, which launched the family fortune.

Abigail ran her finger along the spine of several books, stopping to pull one off the shelf. She read the title aloud. "*Domestic Medicine, or Poor Man's Friend, in the Hours of Afflication, Pain and Sickness.*"

"I know that book," I said. "We spent many hours with Dr. Gunn when he was writing it. Agatha Hollows shared her recipes with him and he with her. Dr. Gunn believed that medicine should be demystified. He wrote his practical guide for folks who didn't have access to a medical doctor. Agatha Hollows would smile politely and patiently as she listened to his modern ways, but when the mountain folk got sick, they would come to her."

Abigail flipped through some pages and then set the book back in its place. She climbed up the spiral staircase, up to the catwalk pulling books out at random, flipping through their pages. I walked around the desk. There was a scent that seemed out of place among the exotic woods, linseed oil, leather. It was a very old scent. Mrs. Twiggs had told me many times how Vanderbilt was a scholar of mysticism and the occult. His wife hosted séance salons on Thursday evenings, often inviting dignitaries from around the world. I could sense the remnants of those séances seeping through the halls, lost souls like Wesley who refused to move on.

"Terra, I found something." Abigail flew down the stairs, holding a small leather-bound volume. "Look." She opened it. "It's his secretary's journal. It has a list of contacts for the opening of the Fillmore Hotel. It says there is to be a big gala on October 31."

"All Hallow's eve." I interrupted her. "All Hallow's eve dates back to the Celtic festival of Samhain. It marked the end of summer and the beginning of the dark cold winter. The Celtics believe that on All Hallows eve, the night before their New Year, which starts on November 1, that boundaries between the worlds of the living and the dead became blurred. It is the night when they believe the ghosts of the dead return to earth. They believe that the Druid and Celtic priests could predict the future on this night."

I could hear Abigail's goose bumps popping. She continued reading, describing the dinner and dance according to the detailed instructions handwritten in the notebook. The evening's festivities were to conclude with a séance led by Madame Claire Renee from New Orleans.

"That name is not familiar to me. Is there anything else about her?"

"No, just a grocery list of sorts that Vanderbilt dictated to his secretary, requirements for accommodations and her carriage. This is interesting. She wants a midwife on call."

"Let me see."

Abigail placed the journal on the coffee table. I pawed through the pages, reading past the menu for the dinner, the seating chart. The last page held several unusual requests by Madame Claire Renee, including bound twines of oak, ash, and thorn. Abigail read with me. "Was she a witch, Terra?"

"That's yet to be discovered. She was, however, trying to unveil someone's true light, someone who was also an honored guest at the hotel."

Abigail pulled out her iPhone. I could see her Google Madame Claire Renee, 1880 New Orleans. "There's nothing about her."

"No you won't find any information on Madame Claire Renee. Renee is a witch's word for seeker. It was her alias."

"Why would George Vanderbilt, the wealthiest man in the world, request Claire Renee, a medium, when he could have hired the world's greatest ghost hunters?" Abigail showed me another book she had found titled *There is No Death* by Florence Marryat and another book *Spirit World*. "This Marryat seems to have written the book on summoning spirits."

I knew all about summoning spirits. I had attended some of the Vanderbilt séances, watching from the shadows, hoping I would connect with some of my coven. I had met Miss Marryat and not thought much of her. "Miss Marryat believed spiritualism was a religion much like the other mediums of that era Maria Hayden and Emma Harding Britten. All of them set standards for the British National Association of Spiritualists. All of it nonsense. George Vanderbilt was a practical man, a mechanical man, that's why he hired the brilliant Olmsted. He would not have hired a spiritualist. He would have hired someone who considered spiritualism a science like Arthur Conan Doyle or Lewis Carroll or Kipling even Elizabeth Barrett Browning. They all believed that the resurrection of the spiritual body could be achieved in a séance using the scientific method. Such a man as the brilliant scientist, Sir William Crookes, is the type of man George would have hired.

Crookes discovered thallium. He was convinced about the reality
of spiritual phenomenon. He devised all sorts of machines to capture spirits and contain them. He was a member of the ghost club.
None of his devices worked, of course. A spirit can't be captured
or caught with gears and vacuum tubes. A spirit is an electrical
impulse. Energy cannot be destroyed only changed. When your
energy, your life force, leaves your physical body, it transforms
into pure light. George Vanderbilt would not be easily fooled by
smoke and mirrors. He'd want hard evidence. He'd want scientific
research. There were many charlatans in his age, looking to peek
into the next world. Claire Renee may have known how to open
the window. At least George thought she could."

Abigail carefully turned each page of the brittle journal. "Is there
anything else about Claire? Or about the night of the opening?"

"Nothing about Claire but there are some notes from an earlier
entry. On September 2, Vanderbilt met with some of the arborists."
Abigail stopped and glanced up at me.

"What's wrong?" I asked.

"Vanderbilt met with a Mr. Foret."

"Yes, that must have been one of Lionel's relatives who came up
from Louisiana during the yellow fever outbreak. Abigail, go get
the curator," I urged her. "Ask her if there is a ledger for the workers. There must have been records kept of staff." I waited under the
desk. Abigail returned shortly with the young woman who had let
her in the private study.

She placed a large ledger on the desk and said, "As you can
see, there are thousands of entries. They kept extensive records of
every employee, including all the day workers as well every piece
of material used."

"What's this line here? Railroad ties?" Abigail asked.

"That's an interesting story," continued the curator. "George Vanderbilt hated trains and everything to do with them. He thought
them large and dirty even though that's how his grandfather made
his fortune. Cornelius Vanderbilt borrowed one hundred dollars
from his mother when he was a kid. He bought a rowboat and
started ferrying people across New York Harbor, which became
the Staten Island Ferry. After building a successful steamboat
monopoly, he turned his attention to railroads. He bought small
lines, connecting them. Before Vanderbilt, it took passengers sev-

enteen different trains to go from New York to Chicago, but he made it possible by one train line. When they started bringing material for the Biltmore, George insisted that he didn't want a railroad, but the architects convinced him he had no choice. He agreed on the condition that the railroad be immediately removed after construction."

"Here this is the name I was looking for—Foret," Abigail said.

"Yes, Foret started as a day laborer. You can see from his pay, which reflected that of a common worker. I noticed this before. His position changed after his first year working with Olmsted. Mr. Olmsted must have thought highly of him to promote him so many times, and his pay steadily increased." The curator ran her finger along the lines of the ledger. "First-class steamship fare for Mr. Foret, Mr. Olmsted, and several others to Ireland. Olmsted took him along to pick out saplings for Biltmore Forest. This was a great honor. Mr. Olmsted kept a close circle around him when it came to important projects."

"Anything else about Foret?"

"He had a house in Biltmore Village, rent free, with some of the other artisans. That's really all there is. If you really want to know more about Biltmore Village, ask our Mrs. Twiggs; she's the expert."

Abigail thanked the curator for her help while I snuck back inside her backpack. "What do we do now?" Abigail whispered to me.

"We go see Mrs. Twiggs."

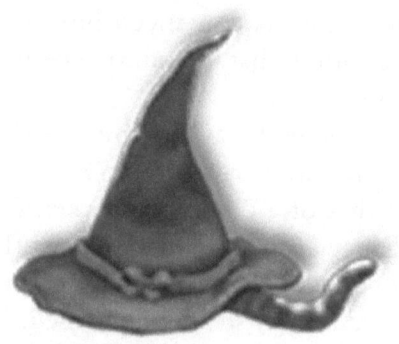

THE RECKONING

MRS. TWIGGS GREETED US AT the door. Pixel flung his paws around my neck, biting me. I had gotten used to his exuberant greeting. Tracker circled around Abigail, wagging his tailless butt and whining. Both were still a bit angry about being left behind. I couldn't chance concealing two of us in Abigail's backpack. Tracker wasn't pleased either. He did not like to let Abigail out of his sight. I was amazed at how attached he had become to her in such a short time.

"So, Abigail was it a success? Did you find what you were looking for?" Mrs. Twiggs asked.

"Everyone was very helpful. Thank you for hooking me up," Abigail said.

"Why don't you come in? I'm closing up. We can have an early supper and you can tell me what you found out."

Pixel followed Mrs. Twiggs into the kitchen, his swinging belly scraping the floor. I would have to be sterner with him and with the humans who constantly met his demands for food. Mrs. Twiggs returned with a tray loaded with melted cheese sandwiches. She placed them on one of the larger café tables and then went back to the kitchen to retrieve soup bowls steaming with homemade tomato bisque. Pixel reached his paws to the edge of the table just able to peek over the top to see the gooey Gruyere cheese melting over the freshly baked French bread. "Me hungry," Pixel said.

Mrs. Twiggs must have learned some cat because she immediately gave Pixel a taste of her sandwich. Abigail threw down her backpack and plopped down on the wooden chair across from her.

"Oh, I almost forgot, silly me," Mrs. Twiggs said, leaping out of the chair with surprising agility for a woman of her girth. She came back carrying two bowls, which I could smell to be tuna fish. She placed them on the table. Pixel leapt onto her lap and then somersaulted onto the table, devouring his bowl before I could even start. I eyeballed the deep red bisque with homemade croutons floating across the sea of goodness. My memories told me it would taste good, but my feline craving drew me to the tuna fish. I truly hated being a cat.

Abigail ate her sandwich, occasionally dipping it into the bisque. Mrs. Twiggs waited patiently until she could wait no longer.

"Abigail, dear, have you had enough?"

"Yes, thank you Mrs. Twiggs." She folded her napkin in her lap. "Your curator friend was very helpful. She let us into George Vanderbilt's private study. We found his secretary's notebook detailing the planning for the opening of the Fillmore Hotel. Vanderbilt invited a medium from Louisiana, a Madame Claire Renee."

"That name sounds familiar," Mrs. Twiggs said, bustling off through the kitchen. I could hear her footsteps going down the rickety wooden stairs into the basement. She returned momentarily, wiping away cobwebs from her face and shoulders. She placed a small leather-bound book on the table in front of Abigail and opened it. "This building we're in was originally a boarding house for some of the artisans." As Mrs. Twiggs recounted what she knew, I found myself drifting off. This was another part of my feline being. I was often sleepy. Pixel leaned his warm body against mine, his belly rumbling in soft purrs.

"Nothing." She closed the book with a thud. I jerked my eyes open to hear the rest of the conversation, but it was no use. I gave in to the sleep.

"This day of our lord the thirtieth of October, 1692, we call this trial to order. Honorable Magistrate Jonathan Goodall, Sr., presiding." The small public house was standing room only. I could smell the anger. I hid in a corner. In the first row, Jonathan Goodall Jr. sat quietly staring straight ahead at his father, nervously checking the time. Any minute his beloved would be dragged in. From the back of the overcrowded room a door flew open. Two men dragged

Elizabeth by her arms, bound in chains. Her beautiful dress torn and dirty. Her hair matted and tangled. "Witch, witch." The crowd spewed venom at her as she was dragged before them. Elizabeth brushed against Jonathan as they dragged her to the front. They chained her to the witness bench. All around me the village folks, most friends at one time of Elizabeth's—people she had known all her life, people she had treated with her compassion and skills—turned on her as they shared stories of her evil doings. All of them lies, a spark that spread burning through the town. Elizabeth was the source of all their bad fortune.

"Quiet, quiet." Jonathan Goodall, Sr., raised his hands, settling the mob. Elizabeth showed no fear. She stared blankly at her accusers. She knew the outcome was inevitable. She would not give them the satisfaction of a single tear. "Elizabeth Oakhaven, you have been charged with practicing witchcraft, sorcery, and consorting with the devil. How do you plea?"

Elizabeth was silent.

"Your silence confirms your guilt. Speak up now if you wish to live."

Cats can't cry. It's not in their physiology. I tried. Angry as I was at Elizabeth for turning me into what I was, I still loved her deeply. My mind raced with all the scenarios of how I could save her. If I only had some magic left. The crowd became louder, chanting, "Burn the witch. Burn the witch."

"Quiet, quiet," Jonathan Goodall, Sr., commanded, banging his gavel.

Then Elizabeth spoke. "Will you grant me my choice of death?"

The good people of Salem shouted, "No."

"Quiet, let her speak," the magistrate said, peering over at her over his glasses.

"You put all my friends, innocent children, young girls to the fire. I wish to be hanged by the neck until dead so as the last sight I see are my dear friends and neighbors as I leave this world."

The courtroom became dead still. At that moment I knew Elizabeth's spirit would move on. There was still hope for me. If she was saved from the real death, the fire, only her body would be lost. I would find her. Elizabeth gazed at her love, her only love. With tears in his eyes, he opened his mouth to speak, but what could he say to persuade his own father—who was killing the mother of his grandchild he would never know. For whatever reason—whether the conviction in Elizabeth's voice or what witch power she had left in her—the magistrate agreed to her request.

As they dragged Elizabeth out, she stopped before reaching the door and turned her head quickly, staring right at me.

She read my mind and saw everything. The water rushing around me in the cave, my transformation, all of it. My childish anger was gone replaced by the great love I had always held for her. She smiled as she was pulled toward the door.

Jonathan Goodall, Jr., rushed to her side. "Wait," he urged the guards. He grabbed Elizabeth by the arm. "This is your last chance. Save yourself."

Elizabeth bent her head near his ear and whispered. Then they took her away.

As I woke, Mrs. Twiggs was still thumbing through the pages of the book she brought up from the basement. "No mention of Claire Renee, but I know I saw that name before. The best way to find out more about her is to check out the other shops. Most of the business owners can tell you the history of their building," I heard Mrs. Twiggs say as I yawned. "Some of the stores will be open late. We can walk around now."

I stood up, stretched, and followed Abigail and Mrs. Twiggs down the uneven cobblestone sidewalk. Some of the stones were sharp and cut into my paws.

We stopped at the first cottage, now home to a dress shop. Its exterior bore a similar resemblance to the Leaf & Page. While some design elements varied, all the cottages were constructed from brick, stucco pebbledash and wood timber so as to recreate Old World charm in this idyllic New World town.

Pixel and I waited outside the shop. Tracker followed Abigail and Mrs. Twiggs. Ashevillians allowed dogs complete access. I've never seen a community that valued dogs as much as Asheville. We walked up and down the block, watching them speak with each store owner. As it grew dark, Mrs. Twiggs sat down on a bench in front of the jewelry store.

"I'm sorry, all. I've gotten a bit worn out. Perhaps we can start this over tomorrow."

The jeweler stepped out on to the small brick porch about to close up for the night. "Just one more," Abigail said, darting up the stairs to talk to him. "Excuse me?"

The old man turned around. "I'm sorry, miss, I'm closing up."

"Actually I didn't want to buy anything. I wanted to ask you a couple of questions if I could."

"About what?"

The old man peeked over Abigail's shoulder at Mrs. Twiggs, who was waving at him. He recognized her and waved back. "Have a seat," he said to Abigail.

They sat on the small wooden bench on the front porch. "I wondered if you could tell me about this building, a little of its history."

"Oh, of course. You know it's one of the original cottages. The local doctor lived here. I've got some photographs and some of his medical journals we found in the attic when we were restoring it."

"Could I see them?" Abigail asked.

He unlocked the door. Abigail waved to us to follow. They walked into a small parlor off to the side of the showroom. I laid down behind the sofa and listened in. Abigail paused to study the photos on the wall by the front door. Some depicted the construction of the village. She stared at one showing children gathered on the village green.

The old man turned. "That's from the day when Teddy Roosevelt came to visit. The man who lived here was Dr. Zachary Rytera. He moved here from Boston because his young son had breathing issues. They came for the clean air. After his wife died, he and his son lived above his office. The rest of the rooms were rented out to the construction workers."

"I'm trying to find information about a Claire Renee or Randall Foret," Abigail said.

He reached next to the couch and pulled out an old leather doctor's bag. Inside was a notebook. "He kept very extensive notes on all his patients. If Claire or Randall lived in the village, more than likely at some point they were patients of Doc Rytera." He skimmed the handwritten pages. "Here's a note about Claire Renee. The doctor treated her for burns." He read silently. "Oh, oh dear. She died during childbirth. Complications from the fire at the Fillmore. I have some more photographs. Perhaps she is in one of them." He placed a stack of old photographs on the coffee table and then he said, "Excuse me for a minute. I'll be right back."

As soon as he left the room, I jumped onto the coffee table and pawed my way through the photos until I found one of several people sitting around the dining room table. One of the men resembled Lionel. Sitting next to him was a beautiful young woman who was the spitting image of Elizabeth. I found another photo of her, a close-up revealing a golden amulet around her neck, its entwined oaks scrolling around a full moon—Elizabeth's amulet. It had been handed down to Elizabeth on her wanding day, and she never took it off until she gave it to her newborn daughter. The old man returned to the room. "Did you find anything?" he asked.

"This is her." Abigail held up the picture.

He looked in the doctor's notes. "Wait a minute. I remember reading something about a young woman." He thumbed through the pages and read aloud. "Mr. Vanderbilt has asked me to board her until her accommodations at the hotel have been secured and make her welcome. There is something peculiar about this young woman. Randall Foret has taken a special liking to her. It caused quite an uproar in the community whereas I have no ill will toward the freed slaves. In fact, I find Mr. Foret to be a gentleman and I hold him as a friend. Others in the community, however, are outraged by the mere thought of these two being associated together. Talk has spread of Miss Renee's condition and that association."

"Is there anything else?"

"There's a letter from Foret dated some years later." He skimmed the letter. "It says he is established and of good health. He has recently married, and his wife has borne him a son. The girl, Claire's daughter, Isabella, is living with him. It appears they moved back to Louisiana." The old man took his glasses off and closed the book. "Many of the cottage owners took in boarders while the hotel was being completed, but they were segregated. Mr. Foret must have been an important man to be allowed to have lived here."

The lights in the room flickered. I felt a chill, the fur on my back raised. Then the lights flickered again and then went out. One by one the streetlights exploded, sending shards of glass onto the cobblestone. I ran out to see Mrs. Twiggs covering her face. Pixel and Tracker hid under the bench. Every store on the block went dark. The only light was the crescent moon filtering through the gabled rooftops. From above the trees I could hear the flapping of wings and a bloodcurdling screech. Tracker ran to the porch and circled Abigail growling. Pixel leapt on top of me. "What's going on?" Abigail screamed.

A burst of air flooded the street, sending off car alarms, snapping off side mirrors like they were twigs. The sound was deafening. Mrs. Twiggs covered her ears with her hands. Tracker howled. The storekeeper screamed above the roar, "It's a tornado."

But I knew different. The reckoning had found us.

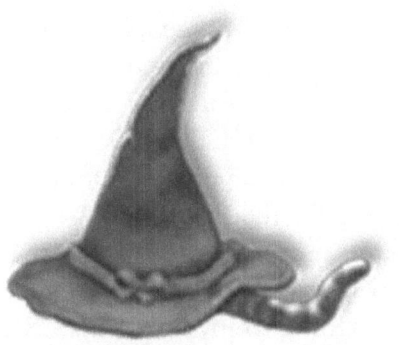

WE BECOME NINE

W E SPENT THE NIGHT HUDDLED around the hearth in the cabin. Mrs. Twiggs joined us. I thought it safer to be out of town at least for the night. We were safe for the moment surrounded by the stream and the power of Agatha Hollows. She had known this day would come, so she had fortified her plot of land with every ounce of magic she had in her. Abigail shook, not from the cold but from the realization that there was nowhere for her to run to. She finally understood what I had been trying to tell her. That we draw the battle line here in Asheville. Mrs. Twiggs was sound asleep with Pixel on her lap and Tracker lying across her feet. I felt no such comfort. Sleep eluded me. I recalled my last dream of Elizabeth. The dream I had a thousand times. I had learned through the centuries that dreams hold meaning. The meanings of this dream, however, eluded me. The images flooded around my head like wild finches feeding on thistle. Flashes of color and constant movement but always in the same sequence. My dreams followed a pattern of my life, starting with the night of my turning and ending with the worst part; the snapping of Elizabeth's neck. I did not need that dream tonight. I did not want it. I could see Mrs. Twiggs tossing and turning in her rocking chair. She, too, had uneasy dreams. Abigail stoked the fire and sipped her tea, a very strong ginger and nettle combination. We sat quietly throughout the night, staring at the fire, not saying a word.

It was now predawn. Darkness of night before the light. That time of morning where you sit and reflect on your life and the choices you've made. Then Abigail spoke. "Why can't you stop this, Terra?"

I looked at her. "When I turned, I lost all my powers."

She stoked the fire again. "How do we fight this thing?"

I wished I had an answer for her. The reckoning had come more quickly than I had expected. The coven was not complete.

Abigail sat back down, tapping her foot rapidly. Then she gathered some kindling for the fire.

I had sensed our ninth Wiccan was in Asheville, but I could not sense her. As dawn broke, I allowed my eyes to close, a quick catnap I thought, laughing to myself: Catnap. Seconds later I opened them to see Pixel an inch away from my face. He whispered, "Terra, look." He turned around. A puff of white smoke rose from the fire and surrounded Mrs. Twiggs. Her eyes flew open. She sprang from the rocking chair and floated to the ceiling of the cabin, her arms outstretched. I smelled the bundle of ash, oak, and thorn Abigail had thrown in the fire. Mrs. Twiggs floated down and stood in front of us. Her aura shone bright white and amethyst purple. I had never seen those two aura colors together. Mrs. Twiggs was a very powerful Wiccan. She smiled as though a shadow had passed from her. She put her hand on Abigail's shoulder. I understood now what Abigail had figured out on her own. Black magic had kept Mrs. Twiggs from turning in Asheville. Our coven was complete.

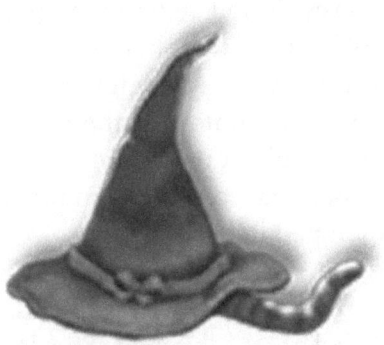

MRS. TWIGGS

"**M**RS. TWIGGS, CAN YOU UNDERSTAND me?"

"Terra, your voice is as I had imagined it. The voice of a young woman."

"I was seventeen when I took this form."

"I don't understand. Why can I hear you now? Why do I feel so strange?"

"The night you drank the potion that should have made you turn, a spell was cast over you to prevent your turning. The black magic surrounding Asheville knew you would be our ninth Wiccan and allow us to close the coven. It had to stop you, but when Abigail burned the oak, ash, and thorn, it revealed your true light, and the good magic of this place allowed you to turn," I told her.

"All these years I felt like there was something missing from my life. Don't get me wrong. I've led a good life. I had a wonderful family and a wonderful husband, but I felt there was more purpose to me. I feel that now."

"The reckoning came for you last night in Biltmore Village. It came for all of us, but I think you were its purpose. It wanted to stop the completion of the coven."

Mrs. Twiggs warmed her hands by the fire. I noticed the snow-white streak in her raven black hair. She stepped lightly almost gliding as she walked. She stared into the dying embers. "Terra, there's a black witch in Asheville." She turned from the fire. Her eyes flashed brilliant opal white filled with milky clouds. She stared into the distance and spoke as if in a trance. "She walks among us yet we don't see her. She helps the black magic. She wants to kill us all." Then her eyes cleared and filled with kindness. I knew she had the power of premonition, but she had not learned how to use it or understand how far in the future she was seeing. It could be one hundred years from now or the present. Until she learned how to control it, I couldn't be sure of her prediction.

Mrs. Twiggs, exhausted from the turning, sat back down in the chair, and Pixel jumped in her lap.

"Mrs. Twiggs, you rest. I will fix us all some breakfast, and we will come up with a game plan," Abigail said.

I followed Abigail to the kitchen. She loaded the stove with firewood and put some salted bacon into a cast-iron skillet. She waited for the sizzle. "Abigail, how did you know Mrs. Twiggs was a Wiccan and what to do?"

"I don't know. I felt like I had to do something. I watched you burn the twigs for the other Wiccans."

It was enough of an answer for now. I could tell how worried Abigail was. I felt responsible. I opened this world of magic to her. Maybe if we had never met, the reckoning would never have come for her, or maybe this was the time we were all meant to be brought together. Witches believe in fate. Each person, Wiccan, or witch is responsible for his or her actions. Those actions determine our fate. We all walk a path to a conclusion, but we can still vary from that path. We all arrive at our final destination. Abigail, Mrs. Twiggs, Pixel, Tracker and myself. We are pebbles tossed into the water, the ripples set into motion and cannot be called back.

We sat and ate our breakfast, each lost in our personal thoughts. After breakfast, we headed into the woods to gather herbs for the coven closing ceremony. Now that we were nine, we would have to swear the oath of allegiance, the same I had recited with Elizabeth and my sisters. Wiccans are witches, what's true for us is true for them. Some witches look down upon them, thought them half-breeds, mongrels, but their magic can be just as powerful. Tonight I will recite the ritual Elizabeth taught me. We will close our ranks, latch our powers together. We will protect Asheville, and more than that, we will save Abigail's life.

Mrs. Twiggs explained many of the herbs to Abigail as they collected them in their baskets. She was well versed in Appalachian folklore and understood the medicinal properties of the plants. Elizabeth had told me that the actual ceremony and reciting of the vows were steeped in tradition, more than actual magic. She said by all of us coming together it made us feel connected, a part of a sisterhood greater than ourselves. She said the only way to defeat black magic is through love and self-sacrifice, caring more about others than yourself, that's the most powerful magic of all. On the surface, the ladies of the Biltmore Society did not seem to hold those values; they seemed quite self-absorbed. If we were to close the coven, they would have to let go of that thinking. The herbs we were collecting would help them with that process. There are only two ingredients that matter. Agatha Hollows had planted mushrooms for such an occasion, part of her Cherokee heritage—peyote—the only ingredient in the potion that actually worked besides a very rare tea leaf. The rest were placebo. Once the ladies drank, they would lose their inhibitions.

"Terra, come here," I heard Mrs. Twiggs call from the meadow that ran alongside the stream.

She stood in a field of wilted milk thistle, black and decaying, rancid smelling. Agatha Hollows had planted this crop to treat liver problems. "No good, no good," Pixel said. I climbed up the tree and looked out over the meadow, which ran for a good half mile into the valley. All I saw was destruction and decay. Finches and thistle, I thought. My dreams had been filled with songbirds.

Mrs. Twiggs gathered up some of the dead thistle. She explained to Abigail, "It looks like all the nutrients have been drained out of them. Usually thistle grows in good soil unattended."

I smelled the dirt. It smelled foul. I followed the path out of the meadow up the side of the mountain. There was black fungus on the birch trees, the elm showed sign of elm disease, all the trees surrounding the cabin were in distress. Scattered in the field lay hundreds of dead yellow finches. I ran back to Mrs. Twiggs and Abigail. "We must hurry. We must hurry the ceremony."

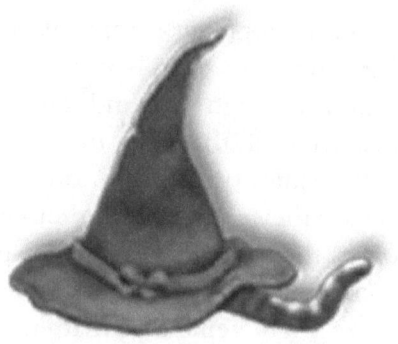

KAREN OWEN

"KAREN OWEN, THAT'S HER NAME, but you must let me do all the talking," Mrs. Twiggs said as we hurried down a back alley in the Montford district. I shivered as we passed through the cemetery. "On occasion, Mrs. Owen sources very rare exotic teas for my shop."

"What do you mean?" Abigail asked.

"Karen had a shop of her own in Vancouver many years ago. She was what is known in the tea world as a tea sommelier. In fact, one of the best in North America. But she's a bit eccentric. She's very temperamental when it comes to her tea talk."

Abigail turned to me and asked, "And we need this tea for the ceremony?"

"Elizabeth was insistent," I told her. "The ritual goes back thousands of years. It has changed through the centuries as it was passed down. The Celtics and then Druids believed that in order for the ceremony to work, the potion needed to break through the blood brain barrier, the membrane that separates the brain from the blood flowing around it. It protects the brain from harmful substances, but in this case to bind the coven we must break through that barrier to unite one mind, one body."

"And this tea leaf helps with breaking through that barrier?" Abigail asked, shifting Pixel in her arms. He had insisted on coming with us.

"That's what Elizabeth told me. I only know the night I drank the potion, the night of the ceremony, I felt that I was no longer an individual but a part of a greater whole. I think it wise not to vary from that potion."

"Here we are." Mrs. Twiggs stopped in front of a long walkway leading up the hill to a yellow Victorian with a wraparound front porch and a large tower in the center. Two iron gargoyles guarded the entry; I felt their stare as they let us pass. The front walkway was adorned with toothless jack-o'-lanterns and colorful fall mums. As we stepped closer, I could see the fine scrolling details milled into the woodwork. I had been here when the craftsmen worked on this house back in the 1890s. By the front door leaned what I imagined Mrs. Owen thought were witches' brooms with crooked and bent hickory handles and straw bottoms tied with twine. A brass plaque next to the front door read, "Owen House Bed-and-Breakfast."

"This is on the Asheville historical registry. It was originally owned by one of the head arborists of the Biltmore Estate," Mrs. Twiggs said.

As Mrs. Twiggs explained the history of the home, Pixel and I stared at the man rocking in the chair at the end of the porch. He was dressed in a frock coat. At first I thought he was one of the Halloween decorations, but then he removed his pocket watch, clicked it open, and wound the stem. I glanced back at Abigail and Mrs. Twiggs. Neither one could see the man.

Mrs. Twiggs rang the doorbell. The heavy oak door swung open. Before us stood a beautiful dark-haired woman with luminescent white skin, her dark blue eyes sparkled with recognition. She smiled and shook Mrs. Twiggs's hand. "Karen, thank you for seeing us with such short notice."

"Not at all. I'm quite intrigued by your asking, Beatrice. Please come in." We filed into the hall, which still had its original mahogany floors and large columns separating it from the parlor. The original crystal chandelier dangled, illuminating the dark wood and an intricately scrolled grandfather clock chimed the top of the hour. She seemed neither bothered nor alarmed by two cats following the humans into the house. Her black-and-white cat, on the other hand, was not pleased to see us. The creature hissed and swiped a paw at Pixel, who ran and hid behind me. "Stop this nonsense, Squirrel," Mrs. Owen said. The creature hissed.

The black-and-white cat looked at me and said, "Squirrel."

"You're not a squirrel, you're a cat," I told it.

"Squirrel is my name," the cat repeated.

"Very well then this is Pixel and I'm Terra. We're friends."

Squirrel pranced around Pixel sniffing tentatively and then stopped, rubbing its head against Pixel, who fell to the floor laughing. The two took off running up the wide staircase. Mrs. Owen noticed the ruckus and bent down staring me in the eye. She lifted me off the ground. "This is a pretty girl," she said over her shoulder to Mrs. Twiggs. "Terra, is it?" she asked looking at me.

I fell silent. How did she know my name?

"You look like a Terra," she said without moving her lips.

I screeched and wiggled out of her grip. I ran up to the top of the stairs. She smiled up at me and then returned to talking to Mrs. Twiggs.

"Bea, I think I have what you need. It's not quite exact but depending on your purpose it may be sufficient." Mrs. Owen knew the purpose of the tea. Of that I was sure. They walked into the parlor and sat in front of the fire. I looked about the room from my vantage point. It had remarkably not changed much since its construction. Some of the furniture was original, I thought. A face pressed against the windowpane near the front door. It was the rocking chair man watching me watching Mrs. Owen. He wasn't the first ghost I had seen in Asheville, but something about him troubled me. I found my courage and quietly walked down and settled on Mrs. Twiggs's lap by the fire.

"Oh, I'm so sorry, Karen, this is Abigail. She's staying with me."

"Oh, family?"

"Of a sort," Mrs. Twiggs replied.

"This is a beautiful house you have," Abigail said.

"Thank you, dear, I bought it when I moved to Asheville. I had to do a lot of restoring to return it to its original glory. Mrs. Twiggs has been a tremendous help; researching records and old photos to make sure everything is period correct. We both share the love of the leaf. Speaking of which." Mrs. Owen jumped up and ran out. She returned with a small wooden box. I recognized the engravings on the lid. They were Druid. She turned the box toward Mrs. Twiggs and opened it slowly. I could smell the essence of blueberry, a very rare tea leaf found on a small Indonesian island. Elizabeth had brought some with her from Ireland.

"How did you find this?" Mrs. Twiggs asked.

Mrs. Owen slapped the lid shut and smiled. "I have made many connections throughout the years in the tea world."

I began to understand who or what Mrs. Owen was. She was a witches' apothecary. Mrs. Twiggs had not known it, but she was drawn to Mrs. Owen for that purpose.

In our village back in Salem we had such a woman who could procure specialty herbs that were not native to the Eastern Seaboard. She traded with pirates and Native Americans, as they are now known. Mrs. Owen was neither a black nor white witch, but a witch she was. She traded in needful things, each having a price greater than its worth. She knew what the tea was used for: one purpose and one purpose only, a coven binding ceremony. My unease about the rocking chair man was well earned. He was different than the other ghosts I had met as he was bound to Mrs. Owen. I wondered what need she granted him. The thought frightened me. She smiled down at me letting me know she understood that I understood.

"Karen, thank you so much, I can't tell you what it's for. Let's call it a personal favor for me," Mrs. Twiggs said.

Mrs. Owen smiled. "You know you must be quite careful. It's a very strong leaf. You must dilute it before drinking. Ten parts hot water to one."

"What do I owe you for this?"

"Nothing but perhaps a favor."

"Of course, anything I can do."

"Let's keep it for another time."

"Thank you so much."

I leapt off Mrs. Twiggs's lap and ran up to retrieve Pixel. I found him and Squirrel rolling down the upstairs hallway. "Pixel, we must leave."

"Squirrel, me like Squirrel."

"Yes, Squirrel is very nice, Pixel, but we must leave." I felt the urgency to leave the house. Mrs. Owen knew me, and with familiarity comes great risk.

Mrs. Twiggs hugged Mrs. Owen in the doorway. She and Abigail started down the steps. Pixel behind. I heard a voice behind me. The rocking chair man stood next to Mrs. Owen. She crouched down and whispered in my ear. "Be careful tonight. The reckon-ing is coming for you." The door swung open, and she lifted off the ground, flying backward into the house. The door slammed shut. The rocking chair man walked along the porch lighting the candles inside the jack-o'-lanterns. As he touched each pumpkin, a black vein of decay spread over the skin. The toothless grins shriveled up into themselves. I ran from the porch.

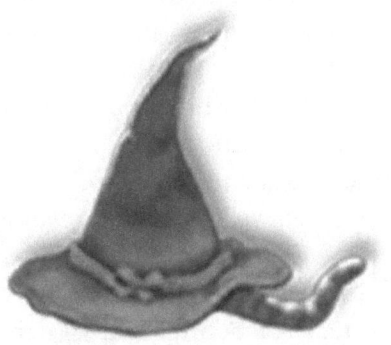

THE CIRCLE

I STOOD IN THE CENTER OF the circle. The Asheville nine held hands. Abigail walked the circle, with a tray of potion. Each of them took a sip and nodded their head at Abigail as she continued to the next. The harvest moon was a brilliant orange, illuminating the woods behind the cabin. Thousands of stars gazed down with an approving twinkle. I had chosen this spot for the closing of the coven because of the mountain ash that grew on the north corner of the field. Elizabeth had told me once that the humans follow the North Star when they are lost and that witches follow their spirit tree which is always true north. I had not understood the reference, but the urgency of this night compelled me to heed her advice. I felt lost, lost in this body, lost in this world, lost in this time.

Pixel and Tracker watched quietly. I could see the fear in both of them. The only true measure of bravery is to be afraid and yet not to waver. I knew that neither one would waver this night. I said. "Ladies of the Biltmore Society, hear my words, tonight one becomes nine and nine become one." I watched their pupils glow red. It had begun. "You must swear tonight by this full moon that from this moment on you will use your powers only for good." As I spoke, I could see shadows in the shadows gathering. I glanced up at the sky, a dark cloud covered the moon, blocking out the light. "You will recite after me the seven incantations of the coven," I said. "Only for good shall we use our powers, kept secret in shadows and midnight hours."

As they repeated the words back to me, my head began to ache. "Sisterhood joined never bond to break." The ground shook under my feet. I felt that I was slipping into a vision. "Our bond is eternal, eternal our fate." A wind gust shook the trees, and a loud roar filled my head. "We vow to hold sacred both nature and man." I had to scream to be heard above the cawing. Like leaves falling on a blustery October, thousands of crows descended upon us from the tree branches. Their yellow soulless eyes looked into me. The circle broke as the ladies fell to the ground, covering their faces. I felt myself lifted into the air. I could smell the wretched breath of the foul creature. I reached up and scratched it across the face, causing it to release its grip. I dropped onto the dirt with a thud. Tracker circled Abigail, biting, nipping and stomping on any crow that pecked at her. Pixel ran to me, covering my body with his.

"Me save Terra, me save Terra." I could hear the crows tearing into his flesh.

As I glanced up, I could see a murder of crows lifting Mrs. Tangledwood off the ground, struggling with her weight. I yelled to her. She turned her head. I could see the insanity taking her, the absurdity of what was happening to her. They carried her over the treetops and disappeared over the ridge into the darkness. From the north, the owls ascended. Great horned, barn, white, all the keepers of the forest. They tore into the crows, thrashing them to pieces. Then they were gone. Our circle was broken. Mrs. Twiggs lay on the ground, bloody and shaking. The rest righted themselves, checking their wounds.

Mrs. Twiggs screamed. "Terra, Mrs. Tangledwood. Emma, they took her."

"Everyone back to the cabin now," I screamed.

When all were safe inside, Abigail latched the cabin door and placed a board across it. I looked about at the scared faces, all of them waiting for words I couldn't find. This was too much, too much for me without my powers. I was still a seventeen-year-old apprentice. "This is too much, Elizabeth," I said, not realizing I spoke out loud.

Abigail retrieved the emergency medical kit and treated their wounds and hers. Pixel lay by the fire, licking blood off his fur. Tracker stood on the kitchen table, staring out the window. Mrs.

Twiggs looked at me with tears in her eyes. "What are we going to do, Terra? We have to save Emma."

"We can't save her. She's gone."

"We have to find her."

"No, Beatrice, she's gone."

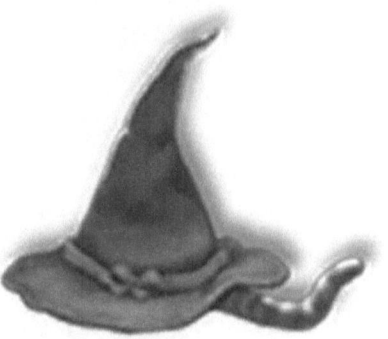

THE AMULET

ABIGAIL AND I WATCHED MRS. Twiggs bustle about the kitchen as she made her scones. We had tried to talk her out of opening the store this morning, but she insisted saying, "It's not what Albert would want." She stopped and stared at his photograph. She was a woman of fortitude. Even with the nightmare of last night, Mrs. Twiggs would not be swayed from her path. There was something very ancient and regal about Mrs. Twiggs. I had not seen it until she turned. She resolved herself to the fact that her friend was gone, that life needed to continue on.

The ladies all scattered to their homes, none of them speaking of the night's events. Although tired and scared, Abigail and Mrs. Twiggs were undaunted. Abigail sat by the fire looking through one of the book of spells. In the short time I had taught her to read Ogham, she had managed to pick it up quite readily. She sat quietly flipping the pages. Pixel and Tracker lay at her feet.

Mrs. Twiggs sat down next to Abigail. "What do we do next, Terra?"

"A hundred and fifty years ago, Claire Renee came to Asheville to hold a séance for George Vanderbilt at the Hotel Fillmore. The night of the séance the hotel burned down. According to the ledgers at the Biltmore Estate, Claire requested twigs of ash, oak, and thorn. She believed black magic was in Asheville and came to destroy it, but the magic destroyed her. At the jewelry store, I saw a picture of Claire. She was wearing an amulet that belonged to my coven leader, Elizabeth. The doctor's note said she never recovered from the fire and died in childbirth. If that amulet is still in Asheville, we need to find it. It's our last hope to defeat the black magic."

"We should go to the historical museum. They have a display on the fire," Mrs. Twiggs said, stroking my soft fur. "Poor, Emma, she loved the museum. She volunteered from the day it opened. Poor, poor Emma."

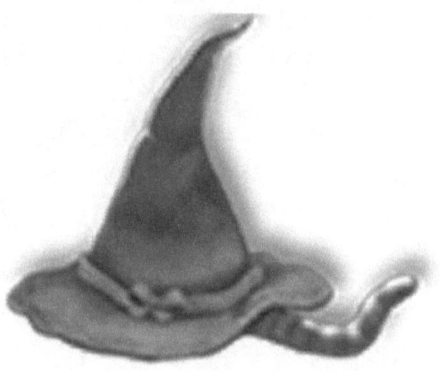

EMOTIONAL SUPPORT ANIMAL

"I DON'T LIKE THIS. I DON'T like it all," I said.

"Sorry, dear, it's the only way."

"I feel like a fool."

"It's just for today."

"Very well then." I reluctantly let Mrs. Twiggs put the emotional support animal vest and collar on me. I have never worn a vest or collar yet pretended to be an emotional support animal. I don't know which part of that sentence bothered me more. Emotional support or animal? I was meant for neither.

"Me too. Me too, emotion animal," Pixel said, climbing up Mrs. Twiggs's leg.

"I'm sorry, Pixel, I could only get one vest. You and Tracker will have to wait here."

"Terra, no go. Pixel, go with Terra." Pixel jumped on my back and bit my neck. The collar itched.

I placed my paws on Pixel's face and rubbed behind his ears. He purred. "I have a very important job for you, Pixel. You must guard the store."

"Me guard store, Terra. Pixel brave."

"Yes, Pixel, you're the bravest cat. No, you're the bravest being I've ever met."

Pixel bit my neck and then jumped up into the front window to keep watch. Tracker stayed velcroed to Abigail. She looked down and whispered in his ear. Tracker laid down underneath the front window by Pixel, letting out a soft moan.

We climbed into Mrs. Twiggs's Volvo and headed to the museum. I sat on Abigail's lap on the passenger side, watching the buildings fly by. We arrived at the Smith-McDowell House, home of the Asheville Historical Museum. Mrs. Twiggs burst into tears when she saw Emma Tangledwood's name on a brass placard hanging in the entryway. I was very familiar with the house as it was Asheville's oldest residence. I was here when it was built, but I had never been inside.

Drying her tears, Mrs. Twiggs explained to Abigail, "The Smith-McDowell House was once home to mayors, Civil War majors and friends of the Vanderbilts. According to legend, it is the most haunted house in Western North Carolina." I wondered if Mrs. Twiggs realized her shop was haunted, but that was a story to tell her another day.

She parked on the street and walked up the steps between the white marble pillars. Wandering in, we flowed through the exhibits, including one on the native landscape. Abigail read the plaque of the first exhibit out loud. "William Wallace McDowell, was born in 1823 in Burke County, which is now named McDowell County. He came to Asheville in 1845 and married Sarah Lucinda. In 1858, they acquired the house and moved in. They had ten children. In December 1859, in response to the raid on Harper's Ferry, he organized a local volunteer company that became known as the Buncombe Riflemen and later joined as an officer in the Confederate Army."

As Abigail read, I recalled meeting McDowell several times while he patrolled the area around Agatha Hollows's cabin. Some of the soldiers stole food from her gardens and some of her livestock, claiming to procure it for the war effort. Agatha Hollows, who had been driven out of Cherokee, North Carolina, held little love for soldiers on either side. The soldiers lived to regret it.

The next exhibit was dubbed the Gilded Age, when the country's uncrowned aristocracy flocked to Asheville for relaxation and leisure.

"Alexander and Elizabeth Garrett bought the house from McDowell in 1881," Abigail read. "The family had originally emigrated from Ireland to America and amassed a sizeable fortune in the Midwest."

As we walked along the exhibits, we came to a display case with a plaque that read, "The fire at the Fillmore Hotel." There was a picture of the hotel's exterior with Wesley standing proudly as guests entered the beautiful marble entryway. The display also held several china plates that were rescued and a ledger. Abigail strolled along, cradling me in her arms. "Stop, Abigail, stop." I pressed my face against the glass. I blinked what must have been several times. In the display of jewelry hung a gold amulet with the oak and blood moon, Elizabeth's amulet.

"What's wrong, Terra?" Abigail asked.

"That amulet. That's Elizabeth's." I stared at it and then gazed at the pictures spread throughout the exhibit. In one picture was the woman Claire, wearing the amulet. "Let me down. Let me down." I ran and hid underneath an armoire.

"What are you doing?"

"Just go. I'll wait here until the museum closes." I hissed at her with the patience of a cat. I thought about the last time I had seen Elizabeth wearing the amulet. It was the night she gave birth. She had handed it to Jonathan to give to her daughter. As the last curator turned off the lights and locked the door, I crawled out of my hiding place. I stared up at the amulet. For more than three hundred years, I had searched for Elizabeth without a clue, and here I was not more than a mile away from her amulet.

"Terra." My blood ran cold as I heard my name behind me.

A white apparition floated down the spiral staircase. I could sense it was a kind spirit. The room smelled like magnolia blossoms, a fragrance I knew from my travels in Louisiana searching for Elizabeth. It was no more than a mist, a vapor but I could make out the form of a woman. "Who are you?" I asked.

"You should know me, Terra. Blood knows blood. You've come here for the amulet. My mother's amulet."

"Claire? Are you Claire Renee?" I paused. "Goodall."

The apparition floated to the ceiling. "I was at one time. Like you I was drawn to Asheville. There's great magic in these woods. Black and white. Now I cannot leave. It holds me. It took my body."

"Who took your body?"

"It took my body as it took my mother Elizabeth."

A shadow passed between us. The smell of magnolias was

replaced by the rancid smell of decaying flesh. "You must go, Terra, it comes."

I pounded on the display case as hard as I could.

"Go, Terra, run, Terra, run." Claire's voice sounded like Elizabeth, so many years ago. I looked above the display case at the lantern that hung overhead. Another item rescued from the Fillmore fire. I leapt onto the case and up to the lantern. Swinging and pulling as hard as I could, I could feel the tether giving. Finally it and I landed with a crash, smashing the glass. I grabbed the amulet in my teeth. As I ran to the front door, something grabbed my tail and pulled me back. My fur smoldered, my flesh began to burn, and then the front door burst open. Mrs. Twiggs stood in the doorway, her eyes blazing red, shining a flashlight to drown out the darkness and light up the room.

"Back and keep the darkness. The light repels you."

I felt the grip release me as I ran to Mrs. Twiggs, who turned and followed me as I ran down the sidewalk.

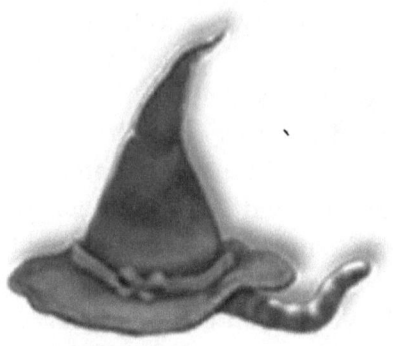

REVELATION

MRS. TWIGGS AND I SAT by the fire at Leaf & Page. Besides the cabin, it was the only place we felt safe. She poured herself some tea with a shaking hand and placed a warm saucer of milk on the side table for me.

"Mrs. Twiggs, how did you know?" I asked.

She put her teacup back on the saucer with a rattle and then took a deep breath. "Terra, I had a vision. I saw everything before it happened. I saw it." She shivered. "I saw Claire Renee, and I saw the creature that keeps her prisoner. I saw you in danger."

A sense of urgency overtook me. "Where's Abigail? Is she safe?" I asked.

"She's upstairs sleeping. She didn't feel well."

"What about the amulet?"

Mrs. Twiggs pulled it out of her pocket and placed it next to her saucer.

"I'll explain later," I said as I ran up the stairs, I leapt onto the bed. Tracker looked up, started to growl, and then realized it was me. He laid his head back down. Pixel never woke. I kissed Abigail's forehead and felt the heat. I took her blanket in my mouth and rolled it down slowly. Her skin was laced with fever blisters. I ran and got Mrs. Twiggs.

She took one look at Abigail. "I'll call the doctor."

"Human medicine won't fix what's wrong with her. Gather the ladies," I said.

It was almost midnight by the time all the ladies arrived. We stood around Abigail's bedside. Gwendolyn Birchbark placed her hand on Abigail's forehead, asking for mercy and compassion to help heal Abigail. Caroline Bowers sat on the edge of the bed. The full moon spilled through the bedroom window illuminating her.

"Terra, she's in her fever dream. I can't reach her," she said.

Each lady summoned what powers they had to help bring Abigail back from the black magic that held her. Mrs. Twiggs entered the room, carrying a teacup. She placed it on the nightstand next to Abigail.

"Terra, I searched all the spell books, and this is the only remedy I could find for Abigail's symptoms. You were right. Her life force is being drained out of her."

I pulled the sheets back. The fever blisters had turned black and crusty. They now covered more than half her body. She was melting away in front of us. Mrs. Twiggs held Abigail's head up, trying to force her to sip the tea. It did not appear to make a difference. She tore a piece of the bottom of her dress off, soaking it in the tea and rubbing it onto Abigail's lips.

"Terra, I don't know what to do." She laid her hands on Abigail's heart and spoke a healing incantation in Gaelic. Abigail stirred and moaned. Her breathing grew shallower.

From the foot of her bed, Pixel cried. Tracker moaned.

"I am a cat," I screamed. "I am a useless feral alley-dwelling creature. I am not Terra Rowan. I am not a witch." I leapt off the bed and crawled downstairs, hiding in a dark corner. "Elizabeth," I whispered. "You have done this to me. You should have let me hang next to you or even more so burned in the final death. I cannot help her." Pixel flew down the stairs, yelling loudly. He slammed into me. "Not now, Pixel. Stop your folly."

"Pixel sad, so sad." His eyes turned as he caught the gleam of the silver chain dangling from Abigail's backpack. He pounced on it, flipping to his back, passing it from paw to paw.

"Stop it, Pixel. Abigail is upstairs dying. You play like the foolish cat you are."

Pixel cried and flipped over, pulling the pocket watch out of the backpack. It sprang open.

"Look what you did," I said with anger. His orange saucer eyes gleamed. "You've broken it." I stepped over and pawed the watch, breaking it open. Inside the back cover I saw the initials JGJ. I thought of Salem, I thought of the courtroom and Jonathan Goodall, Jr. checking his watch. Abigail's family heirloom which was stuck at three, the black witches' hour, the hour that Lionel and Bryson were murdered, the hour that Abigail's parents were taken from her. I grabbed the amulet, carrying it upstairs and placed it on Abigail's chest. If she was who I thought she was, its power would save her. Nothing happened. No magic was left in the amulet or me.

I felt hopeless and sat with the others while we watched over Abigail. We each took shifts throughout the night. I held little hope for the dawn. I glanced around at all the ladies, seeing the sadness in their eyes. What a fraud I am, they must think. If I can't save Abigail, how can I save any of them? I am just a cat. I went out into the alley. This was my life. There was no hope of ever finding Elizabeth, of ever becoming my true self again. My only link to my past a powerless golden amulet from the woman who cursed me to this life and cursed her daughter to be trapped between worlds. This alley is my home, my final destination. I settled down by the dumpster and let sleep take me. In the morning, I would leave this town forever.

With a rush, I was startled awake. I felt myself being lifted off the ground and thrown in a sack. I scratched and hissed to no avail. I was thrown down and could hear the clank of a car trunk closing. I banged, knocking against the sack and the hard metal of my transport. The car hit a bump, and I banged my head inside the trunk. I saw stars, and then the dark took me.

I awoke. I was still trapped in this canvas sack. I clawed and bit at it. My captor tied the bag closed, sealing me off from the light. I could smell the sulfur from the match strike and then the smoke from the fire. It was the true death I had escaped over three hundred years ago.

"No!" I heard a scream and then I felt myself lifted out of the fire. The bag opened. Abigail was standing over me, holding a bloody silver knife. I gasped for air, my eyes burning from the smoke. Ashes and sparks flew into the night as Abigail picked me up.

"Terra, are you okay? Your fur is singed."

"Abigail, how… how are you here?"

She pulled the amulet out from under her blouse. "My grandmother, Claire, came to me in a vision. She told me how to find you, Terra. She told me I'm a witch. The reckoning took my mother, Isabella, and my father. Only I was saved. This tattoo—" She paused. "My father used to call my mother Tinker Bell. I never knew why I was so drawn to the fairy."

I gazed behind Abigail. Claire Renee glided up. She had taken the form of her former body, a beautiful woman who looked like Elizabeth who looked like Abigail. She smiled.

"Now that Abigail has the amulet, my light is released," Claire said. "Keep my granddaughter safe, Terra Rowan."

"Claire, what is the reckoning?" I asked.

"There is great magic here—black and white. I came to destroy one and preserve the other, but the black magic was too strong. If you can't control it, it will control you." Then she rose into the sky and disappeared into a burst of white light.

"I wounded it. I know I did. I looked right at it, but I couldn't see it, Terra," Abigail said.

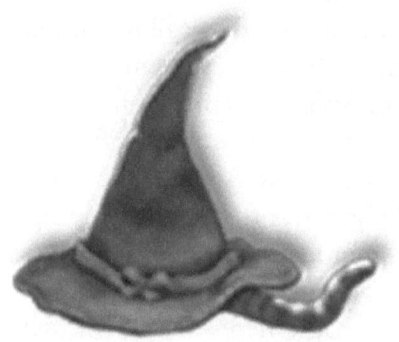

ALL HALLOW'S EVE

MRS. TWIGGS CALLED A MEETING of the ladies of the Biltmore Society. I needed for them to understand the peril they were in and the circumstances that brought them to it. "Servants of the reckoning killed Lionel and Bryson and almost killed me," I said.

"Today is Abigail's eighteenth birthday, her wanding day," Mrs. Twiggs said. "The only chance we have to protect ourselves is for Abigail to turn. She must find her wanding tree. For that reason, I believe we were all brought together. Somewhere here in the Biltmore Forest is her spirit oak."

Mrs. Bowers stood up. "You told us we needed to be a coven of nine, a closed coven. There are only eight of us left. I don't like this. I don't like this at all."

"We're still a coven. We're still a family. We will watch over each other and use our special powers to fight the reckoning," Mrs. Twiggs said.

I walked over to where Abigail was sitting. "Do you feel better? Your fever's broken," I whispered so only Abigail could hear. "It's up to you. You have the Oakhaven bloodline. Only you can save them, save all of us. Even a closed coven of nine could not protect us. We need you."

Abigail squirmed in her chair. "I don't want this, Terra. I don't want this responsibility."

"Your great-grandmother was a very powerful witch. Perhaps as powerful as the old ones. You can do this, Abigail. I will help you."

Abigail smiled. "How do we find my spirit tree?"

Tracker jumped from the front window where he was keeping watch and sat in front of Abigail. Then he let out a bloodcurdling howl. The ladies held their ears. "This is how we'll find your tree, Abigail. Hold out your hand." As she did, I extended my paw and pricked her finger.

"Ouch, what are you doing, Terra?"

I grabbed her hand and put her finger under Tracker's nose. He breathed the scent in, the scent of old blood and old magic. He howled and ran to the front door. Abigail and Mrs. Twiggs grabbed their coats and some flashlights. I turned to the ladies. "Tonight on All Hallow's Eve, the veil between worlds will be lifted. Leave all the lights on. Put candles in the windows. Lock the door behind us. No matter what happens do not leave this room. Stay in your circle and concentrate all your powers. Concentrate on Abigail's fate. Let your spirits follow us into the woods."

We jumped into Mrs. Twiggs's Volvo. Pixel, Tracker and I sat in the back. Tracker paced back and forth, whining. He had the scent. He stuck his head out the window and let out a low moan.

"Terra, how do you know the tree is in Biltmore Forest and not a hundred miles from here?" Abigail asked from the front seat.

"It was something that your grandmother said to me in the museum. She said she was drawn to Asheville and to the woods. Something in her bloodline drew her to this spot. That same magic brought you here. I've never seen any spirit tree draw a witch as powerful as this beacon has brought you. It must be very old."

"Olmsted brought oak saplings from Ireland." Mrs. Twiggs interrupted. "Mr. Vanderbilt believed they were descendants of the Druid's oak orchards."

"The Wiccans of the Biltmore Society settled in a coven circle surrounding this forest. The tree is here," I said.

"This whole forest was built on mysticism," Mrs. Twiggs said.

Tracker stuck his head out the window and howled. Mrs. Twiggs slammed on the brakes. I flew forward. Pixel tumbled to the floor. We stopped at the guard shack of the entrance to the Biltmore Estate.

"Terra, it's almost eleven," Mrs. Twiggs yelled. Mrs. Twiggs drove through the secret gate on the side and wound around the forest road, her headlights barely illuminating the path in front of us.

"Abigail, we have to find the tree before the New Year. It must be on your eighteenth birthday."

Mrs. Twiggs turned the engine off. As she opened the back door, Tracker flew out and disappeared into the woods, Abigail called after him. "Follow him," I said. We ran in front of the humans, Pixel faster than I. We could see Tracker, a flash of red and white, in the dark, slaloming through the trees. He stopped in an orchard of bamboos. Pixel ran to him. I followed.

Pixel turned, panting. "Tracker, something wrong. Tracker, not good."

Tracker fell to the ground on his side, his back legs trembling. I looked up the towering bamboo trees to see hundreds of crows perched on top of the great stalks. I smelled the air, a wicked wind whistled through the branches. The dark magic was stirring. The reckoning was near. Pixel nuzzled Tracker. "Tracker, get up. Tracker."

I saw flashlights dance behind us. I called out, "Mrs. Twiggs. Abigail." They ran toward my screams. Abigail sat on the ground and put Tracker in her lap, rocking him. She looked up with tears in her eyes.

"What's happening, Terra? What's wrong with him?"

Abigail clutched the amulet hanging from her neck. It glowed at her touch as I had seen it do for Elizabeth. Mrs. Twiggs stood silent; something was wrong. Her eyes turned, flipping over until all I could see was the white. She held her arms outstretched and lifted off the ground, into the trees, into the bamboos.

"Abigail, you must find the tree. It's the only way," I said. "Pixel, stay with Tracker."

Pixel looked up with his orange saucer eyes, his eyes full of love and anger. Anger for the darkness that was taking his friends. His brave heart beat louder than the oppressing wind. "Me stay, Terra, me stay." He lay across Tracker's chest.

"Abigail, come. We must go now," I said. We fought the wind pushing against us.

Abigail screamed over the howling. "I remember Hurricane Katrina. My mother blown away by the winds and the waters. Trees bending, snapping." She yelled over the noise. She picked me up and turned her face to the wind and pushed forward. "Terra, I don't know which way to go. I'm lost."

I screamed, "Head north. Your tree will be north."

Abigail pushed on, branches snapping and tearing at her clothes and face. She held one hand out, slapping the deluge of debris and clutched me with her other. And then above the wind and the snapping branches I heard Abigail sing. She sang her great-grandmother's song, the song of my coven. The words that were sung by the old ones. The words of love, compassion and sacrifice. The wind stopped. Abigail collapsed to the ground. "Terra, it's near. I can feel it. My tree is near. It's calling to me." Abigail scooped me up and ran. Her feet barely touched the ground, fearless and knowing. Even I couldn't see through the complete darkness of the center of this maze of old growth. My head began to spin; the vertigo was taking me. The voices spoke. Elizabeth spoke.

"Terra, my family's spirit tree is the mother of all oaks. Its branches hung over the old ones. Its leaves rustle beneath the feet of the earth walkers. Its bloodline is our bloodline going back four times. I love you, Terra. I will find you."

When I came to, Abigail was breathing heavily, leaning up against a massive oak. Its branches spread a hundred feet in all directions and a hundred feet more to the top. Its roots smelled sweet like freshly cut grass. Abigail hugged the tree, spoke to it in a whisper.

She turned to me. "Terra, what do I do?"

Before I could answer, it appeared. Space and time around it blurred and twisted. A vortex of darkness, their shapeless forms glided through the trees, snapping them like toothpicks. Then it took the form of Mrs. Tangledwood. Abigail grabbed me and held me tight. I screamed, "Don't listen to it, Abigail. Block it from your mind. It will try to confuse you."

Abigail began to shake. Her eyes rolled back into her head. I leapt from her arms and ran toward Mrs. Tangledwood. I screamed. "I know your name. I'm not afraid to speak it."

A graveyard whisper filled my head with a familiar voice. "Speak it, Terra Rowan."

The form of Mrs. Tangledwood gave way to a swirling darkness. Standing before me, my dearest of all my sisters, Prudence Thornwood. "Terra, it is too strong for you. You must submit."

"Prudence, no."

"Terra, I had no choice. It filled my mind with pride and envy.

It promised me great wealth and power."

"No, Prudence."

"Elizabeth didn't love us. She kept the book for herself. Its powers are endless, Terra. I had to tell the secret, Terra. The book possessed me. It possessed me."

"You are not my Prudence," I cried.

Her face contorted. Her master spoke. "Terra Rowan, join us or die the true death." It lifted me off the ground. I turned to see Abigail, arms outstretched, slowly rising up the tree, her back bent. A branch cut her hand wide open, the blood dripped down her side to her leg.

"I fear you not," I said. "You are but shadows and mist." I found myself flying through the air, landing with a thud against the base of the tree. I felt something wet on my fur. Abigail's blood soaked the fur and the ground around me. The tree shook. Roots snapped out of the ground and drank Abigail's blood with a thirst. The darkness approached us.

Abigail screamed. I could hear the oak tree snap high above us, a branch landed in Abigail's hand. She fell to the ground. She kneeled and looked up at the approaching swirl of darkness. Then she glanced at the branch in her hand. "I fear you not. Darkness fear the light. I am Abigail Oakhaven." She raised her wand. An explosion of white light lit up the forest and rippled out through the treetops.

A primordial, guttural voice yelled in agonizing pain. And then it was gone. Abigail turned to me. Her hair silver white, her skin glowed in the dark. She knelt down and scooped me up and hugged me. She rocked me. Near us, Mrs. Tangledwood lay on the ground, the color gone from her face. Her once raven hair gray. She raised her gnarled hand. "It promised me life, Terra. It promised me power." She pulled the book from under her cloak. "It lied to me. I'm sorry."

"I know, Emma. The book controls those who can't control it. The ancient magic reaches out through the pages. It lied to my dear friend Prudence and possessed her the same way it took you. She came to Asheville to destroy the Oakhaven spirit tree, to end the Oakhaven bloodline, but the bloodline continues. Prudence died in the fire, but the book cannot be destroyed. Emma, how did you come upon the book?"

"In the ashes of the Fillmore. I wanted to leave my legacy, to restore the Fillmore, but when I found the book, I had to have it. I didn't mean to kill Lionel or the boy. I had no control."

"I know, Emma. Sleep now," I said. Emma's eyes closed as she let out one last breath.

Pixel and Tracker ran up to us, knocking us over. Tracker licked Abigail's wounds. Pixel grabbed me and threw me onto the ground. "Terra, okay? Terra, okay? Me save Tracker."

"Yes, you did. You're the best familiar a witch could ever have, Pixel."

Pixel smiled.

Mrs. Twiggs stood on the edge of the fallen trees. Her light shined around her, a brilliant purple and white. She had been thrown into the abyss and returned stronger. She hugged us all. When she released the hug, she knelt down next to her dear friend and moaned, "Emma." Mrs. Twiggs went to grab the book.

I screamed. "Stop."

Abigail knelt down and picked up Elizabeth's book of spells, etched on the cover, the barren oak tree with a blood orange moon over it. As she touched the tree, the crest came to life, illuminating her surroundings. Tree branches writhed like in a storm. The book flipped open, and written in blood I could see Prudence Thornwood, 1692; Emma Tangledwood, 2017. The book snapped shut. Abigail tossed it into her backpack.

Pixel said, "Go now? Me hungry."

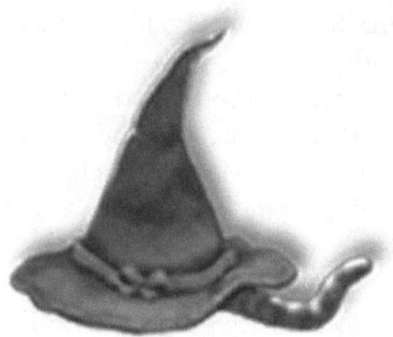

EPILOGUE

I WATCHED MRS. TWIGGS BAKING THE morning scones. She looked over her shoulder with a smile. "They're not going to bake themselves now, are they?"

Pixel begged for crumbs, reaching up Mrs. Twiggs's leg. Abigail sat by the fire, Tracker on her feet.

"Oh dear, look at the time," Mrs. Twiggs said as the cuckoo clock struck seven. She stopped in front of Albert's photograph. "Good morning, dear," she said.

"Good morning, my love," Albert Twiggs replied.

ABOUT THE AUTHOR

AWARD-WINNING JOURNALIST VICKI VASS TURNED in her reporter's notebook to pursue her passion for mystery writing. Her first series, *Antique Hunters Mysteries,* was a finalist in the 2016 Mystery & Mayhem contest. Her travels to Asheville and the Biltmore Estate inspired this tale. Vicki has written more than 1,400 stories for the *Chicago Tribune* as well as other commercial publications including *Home & Away*, the *Lutheran* and *Woman's World*. Her science fiction novel, *Eleven: 1*, draws on her experience in Sudan while writing about the ongoing civil war for World Relief. She lives in the Chicago area with her husband, writer and musician Brian Tedeschi, son Tony, Australian shepherds Atticus and Tracker, kittens Terra and Pixel, seven koi and Gary the turtle. For more about Vicki, go to **www.vickivass.com**.

BOOKS BY VICKI VASS

Antique Hunter Mysteries
Murder by the Spoonful
Pickin' Murder
Killer Finds
Key to a Murder

Neighborhood Watch
The Postman is Late
Gem Hunter

Science Fiction
Eleven: 1

www.ingramcontent.com/pod-product-compliance
Lightning Source LLC
Chambersburg PA
CBHW022113170626
46808CB00002B/716